Sweet Life

EROTIC FANTASIES FOR COUPLES

Sweet Life

Erotic Fantasies for Couples

EDITED BY

VIOLET BLUE

CLEIS
PRESS

Published in the United States by Cleis Press Inc., P.O. Box 14684, San Francisco, California 94114.

Printed in the United States.

Cover design: Scott Idleman

Text design: Karen Quigg

Cleis Press logo art: Juana Alicia

First Edition.

10 9 8

For Todd, my love

Contents

Introduction: La Dolce Vita

La dolce vita—literally *the sweet life* in Italian—has come to represent a life filled with many pleasures. In Federico Fellini's film of the same name, Marcello Mastroianni plays a gossip columnist forever idealizing that which is out of reach: a life of rich pleasures belonging to seemingly everyone but him.

Who hasn't fantasized about living the sweet life—or yearned for a life filled with pleasure and satisfaction? We, too, are always searching for that spark of excitement in life—and when it comes to sex, we want that spark to ignite fires.

Between these covers, you will meet many couples who have embraced the sweet life as more than a lovely phrase. They have made their fantasies into reality—even if only for a delicious moment. Some of these fantasies will be delightfully familiar while others emerge as new and inviting. Each offers up a taste of forbidden need, finally unleashed.

These stories are addictive, hot little reads. Girlfriends and wives try on schoolgirl outfits and strap-ons to discover what they've been missing. Boyfriends and husbands become doctors, headmasters, daddies—or simply do as they're told and emerge more satisfied than ever. Lovers confess dark desires and inspire their partners to act on them; sweethearts scheme and take the upper hand. Couples add a woman, a man, or both to their already hot sexual encounters. Passion consistently takes precedent over taboo. There is *nothing* these lovers won't try for each other, and it's all here in twenty-one expertly crafted, arousingly explicit tales.

The lucky characters in the stories in *Sweet Life* bring their forbidden fantasies into reality in any number of ingenious ways. In some instances, the couple has made a deal: a fantasy for a fantasy. In others, both parties have made a list of their hottest wishes, in order from one to ten, and they greedily start at the top. Others find that one of the pair is a little more gutsy that the other, engaging in subterfuge to make their lover's—and their own—dreams come true in encounters of sticky, breathless success. There are nervous, sweaty, and gratifying first-time threesomes and sex parties. More than a few encounters include power exchange, including a spellbinding spanking scenario, sizzling role-playing and delicious role-reversals. Quite a few of these women strap it on and give it to their guys in charged scenes that practically burn the print off the page. And some outrageous encounters develop spontaneously—even by accident.

I discovered, as I was assembling this collection, that I, too, yearned to find arousing stories that reflected my preferences yet shattered the mold. As I read the stories in this book, I realized that I was one of the folks in relationships who got hot thinking about sexual experimentation, wanted the thrill of the new, the taboo—and to get off reading about it. Suddenly I found myself reading submissions for *Sweet Life* to my husband over an evening glass of wine, or leaving a story suggestively where he likes to drink his morning coffee. The book began to stand on its own, and the stories, it seemed, had many destinies.

The writers who contributed to *Sweet Life* are very hard workers and are seriously naughty for making these nice people do nasty things. Watch out for them. I owe a debt of thanks to my colleague, friend, and partner in crime, Thomas Roche, for advice given (often after the stroke of midnight). My gratitude goes to Felice Newman for support, for her wickedly dry humor, and for relishing an opportunity to take a chance. And to Frédérique Delacoste for being a sweetheart— your tireless work is appreciated. Thanks to Constance Claire for everlasting encouragement. And to my sweetheart, Todd, with whom I will share many moments of discovery.

May you find a life filled with many pleasures.

Violet Blue
Berkeley, California
September 2001

Playing Doctor

DANTE DAVIDSON

"My fantasies are getting stranger," Katie began. Her voice was low, even though it was only the two of us in the room.

"Tell me about them."

"I'm embarrassed, Jack," she said, before instantly correcting herself. "I mean, I'm embarrassed...Doctor."

"Nothing that the human mind produces should embarrass you," I assured her. "There is a reason for everything, every thought, every desire."

This was a more poetic discourse than I usually gave, and Katie turned to look over at me for the first time since she'd taken her position on the burgundy leather couch. I hoped that my blue eyes suggested only an endless reserve of calm and patience and none of the lust that flickered restlessly behind them. Yet lust was what I felt more than anything else. Katie is twenty-four, ten years my junior, but she appears even younger than that. She lay flat on her back, her slender body held rigid, and my eyes lingered over her fine, honey-colored hair, her pert breasts, and the line of her long, bare legs seen through the split of her front-buttoned skirt.

"I'm such a bad girl, Doctor," she said, and her breath caught in her throat. I loved the way those words sounded in her sweet, lilting voice. I wanted to tell her that I knew exactly how bad she was, and I wanted to tell her how fucking hard it made me. But this was her show, and I let her take it at her own pace. Leaning back on the sofa, she explained, "I have these twisted fantasies about going to private school."

"You attended one?" I asked, knowing the real answer, but wanting to hear where she was headed.

"Yes, but these are made-up memories, none of these things actually happened to me." She paused, and I caught the fact that she was blushing. As I made a few hurried scratches on my note pad to give her time, I thought about how much I enjoyed playing games with her. Yet this particular game was going far beyond our normal "doctor/naughty nurse" or "teacher/student" routine. I had the feeling that Katie was really going to tell me a secret.

"I was an average student in real life, rarely praised"— she paused before adding "or punished." Then she was silent once more, as if listening to that word reverberating within our large living room, echoing off the bookshelves and the windows that look out over Manhattan's richest quarter.

"Punished?" I asked her. We'd been circling around this for some time, and I'd waited for her to reveal the all-consuming desire that I sensed lay at the core of our role-playing fantasies.

Fantasies that we acted out, but never to the point of no return, never to the proper finish. When she looked over at me again, her face registered the fright of a young child caught in the act of stealing from the cookie jar, or a teenager sneaking into the house late only to confront the angry visage of a waiting father.

"Go on," I said encouragingly. I prayed that she would be able to bring this secret to the surface, where we might both benefit from the revelation.

"I have fantasies before I fall asleep each night," she said slowly, obviously determined this time to get the whole story out. I was thankful that she did not look over at me right then because it would have broken the atmosphere, the magic spell of our game. I was completely unable to hide the stirring of desire for her that I felt deep in my stomach. And lower.

"I imagine that I am called into the headmaster's office for some infraction. He asks me if I like being a bad girl."

Do you, Katie? I wanted to ask. *Do you like being bad?* But that would spoil things, wouldn't it? She had to tell me in her own way, had to explain what she was feeling.

"He tells me that he is tired of having me sent to him, that I apparently have no respect for the school or my teachers. And he says that I will have to be punished in a more severe way this time, so that it may have a stronger effect on me."

"Is he the one to punish you?" I asked when she seemed unsure of how to continue.

"Yes."

Another pause.

"How?" I waited for her answer with my pen tip poised on the pad.

"He stands up and walks across the room to a couch. He motions for me to follow, and when I come to him he bends me over his lap and raises my short, pleated skirt." She took a breath, and exhaled with a rush of words. "He pulls down my white panties and gives me a hard, sturdy spanking."

Neither of us spoke during the fraction of a minute it took me to compose myself. The image of my nubile darling with her white cotton underpants down to her ankles and her bare bottom flushed from a thorough spanking affected me deeply. I willed my cock to lie still, painfully aware of the growing bulge against my zippered crotch.

"Is that where the fantasy ends?" I finally murmured.

"No," she admitted. "There's more. At first, I try to struggle against him, but he holds me over his lap with an iron grip. He spanks me until I sob—something I haven't done for years. If I cry now, it's silent and discreet," she said, looking at me, and I nodded. I know exactly what she's like when she cries. "But in the fantasy I understand that the headmaster will continue the spanking until my resistance is gone completely. There's something important about that, as if the 'giving up' is as necessary as the pain and the tears."

I'd been scribbling nonsense words on my pad of paper, finding this role-playing act increasingly difficult to keep up. The image of her coming, of her delicate fingers working faster and faster in little circles around her clit while her mind played a wonderful X-rated movie behind her tightly closed eyelids— this image did not help me still my hardened cock. It felt huge, larger than it had ever gotten when we'd played like this before. I think, probably, because the whole encounter felt so real, and that made it feel intensely dirty. Inwardly, I sighed with relief when she kept on without waiting for me to give a response.

"I have other fantasies, too, and I guess, since I've come this far, I ought to tell you everything."

"Yes, I think that would be good," I whispered. She looked over at me, questioning the low, gravelly sound of my voice, and I nodded my head at her, letting her know how much I wanted her to continue.

"Another version has me being bad once again, only this time the school has different rules."

I wrote down "bad" on the note pad, imagining what a real doctor would write in this situation, wondering if another listener would understand that this word was as important to Katie as "punishment" and "spanking." I could guess the other key words from my own fantasies: "naughty," and "discipline." As I made those notes, I wondered how far Katie's masochistic thoughts ran, and I wondered why *we* hadn't gone this far before. We'd dabbled in domination, but not in serious discipline.

Katie obviously hadn't accepted this side of herself, or she wouldn't be telling me, with that worried expression marring her comely features. "Confession" occurred to me, and I wrote it down in the growing list on my pad.

She said, "Those caught misbehaving are sent to the doctor's for an examination. The headmaster says that I am to go to the infirmary, and I walk down a long hall until I reach that part of the school. The nurse ushers me into a stark, white examining room and tells me that I should remove my clothes and put on the white cloth gown.

"Within moments, the door opens up and a handsome doctor, about forty years old, enters the room. He immediately requests that I lie flat on the table on my back, and he puts on rubber gloves and proceeds with a full pelvic exam. I am frightened because I'm turned on and know that he will be able to tell from the wetness, but he doesn't say anything.

"That done, he asks me to turn over. He tells me that he must take my temperature, and that he will do it with a rectal thermometer because that's what he does for naughty girls. This part of the fantasy is so real. I know the feeling of the cold glass thermometer being inserted, know the pressure *there*… I start to cry silently during the long minutes that he leaves the thermometer in place."

She stopped and took a deep breath, and I watched her profile. Her cheeks were flushed the dark red of true shame, and she nervously bit on her bottom lip before she began speaking again. "When he removes the thermometer, he tells me that my temperature is normal, and that I am quite healthy. Then he has me sit up, straightens my gown for me, and asks me if I know what that means. I say that I do, that it means I am in for another spanking over the headmaster's knee. But I'm wrong. He says that he is then required to purge the naughty thoughts from my body and that these thoughts are best gotten rid of with an enema."

She seemed to want to sink into the couch as she told me this, and I wished I could go on my knees before her and stroke her gossamer hair and kiss her cherry lips and tell her in my most soothing voice that everything would be OK. And then, I would like to tell her how very much I was dying to examine her and spank her and join her in each and every naughty, forbidden act that gave her so much pleasure in the private safety of her mind at night, yet brought her guilt in the sunny daylight on the mornings after.

When she didn't continue with the fantasy, I cleared my throat again and asked, "Does he give you an enema, Katie?"

"He gives me the choice," she said, "Whether I would prefer the spanking or the 'purging.' "

"And you choose—?"

She actually turned her head toward the wall when she answered, and I had to strain my ears to hear her tiny voice. "The enema."

"Yes." I couldn't stop the stream of images that flooded through my mind, visions of this anonymous doctor telling Katie to turn on her stomach again and inserting the tip of the black rubber nozzle into her asshole. I longed to part the cheeks of her sweet, heart-shaped ass myself, to spread K-Y Jelly in that split of her body, to administer the "purging" enema to my sweetheart who so desperately wanted to be bad, and to be punished for her naughtiness.

When I realized that she was through talking, at least for the moment, I put my note pad down and stood and walked over to the couch. She was startled and began to sit up, but I shook my head and said, "No, stay there for a moment. Let me talk."

Sitting next to her on the edge of the sofa, I took one of her hands in both of mine. I was aware of the heat radiating from her slim body, of the shine to her eyes, the color in her cheeks. I thought quickly about what I was going to tell her, and I tried to formulate my response into what I imagined a real doctor would say.

"These fantasies worry you." This was not a question, but she nodded anyway, her gold-flecked brown eyes wide open and staring at me. That was a good sign. She was no longer blushing, no longer turning away. She felt what was coming—I intuitively knew that—yet I kept stroking her hand and talking to her in my deep voice, using as soothing a tone as possible.

"They needn't cause you such distress," I told her, hoping that she could see the smile lines crinkle in the corner of my eyes, although my face remained serious. "As I said at the beginning of our session, nothing the mind produces should frighten or embarrass you. These are only thoughts, only fantasies. And you can use them to your own benefit. To your own joy." I could tell from her expression that she liked what I was saying.

"This is not conventional, what I am about to suggest, but I would like to explore your fantasies with you."

Katie smiled. It lit her face from within, and her entire countenance seemed to relax. When she finally spoke, it was in barely more than a whisper, and I realized that she had truly been frightened to reveal her secret to me, no matter that we've been married for four years, or that I've always tried to make her comfortable with her darkest desires.

"Then it's come true."

"What, darling?"

"My fantasy. Because you always play *him* in my daydreams—the doctor, the principal, the headmaster. Jack, you always play 'the man.' "

I couldn't turn back now. After all this time, we were on the verge, ready to plunge into a world where her fantasies melded with mine. I kept her hand tight within my own as I asked, "Katie, tell me the truth. Have you been a bad girl?"

She didn't really need to say the word. I was so ready, ready to move her from her comfortable reclining position on the sofa to a much more suitable one over my knees, her skirt pulled up, her panties down. But I wanted to hear her answer, and I waited until she nodded and in that same, hushed voice said, "Yes, Jack."

"There's only one way that we deal with bad girls, here," I told her, helping her to find her place across my lap. "With a bare-bottomed spanking," I continued, feeling the warmth in her skin as I slid her skirt up her thighs, taking the time to admire her pale bottom cheeks as I lowered her pristine white panties. "You understand," I said before my hand met her ass for the first time. "You do understand, don't you, Katie?"

Her words, "Oh, yes, Jack," were almost orgasmic in quality, a rush of breath as she prepared herself for the feeling of my hand connecting with her skin. I started then, and my cock strained up to press hard against her body as I spanked her. Christ, the feel of it was almost unreal, my hand smacking her blushing skin, her body squirming, rocking hard against my cock. I could have come from that movement alone, the whole image of it, her harsh breath catching in her throat, the clapping sound that my hand made as I continued to spank her adorable ass.

What a pair we made. She was growing wetter each time I landed a blow, and I was getting harder. I didn't even think it was possible for my cock to grow any larger, but I could feel my erection straining, desperate for release.

But there was more. I knew it. I had to stay in control, to part the cheeks of her ass and let my stiffened fingers spank her pussy. Not as hard as I'd spanked her ass. More of a firm love tap than anything else. Yet it was enough for Katie, enough to have her arching to meet my fingers, greeting them with a flood of wetness. I gave her that taste of pleasure before continuing to punish her ripe and cherry-reddened ass cheeks. Playing her, making her cry out but be unsure of what she was crying out for. She wasn't in serious pain, but in serious pleasure. She wanted more, but she didn't know exactly what "more" she wanted.

That didn't matter, because I knew.

Having felt with my fingertips just how wet and ready she was, I moved her off my lap and onto all fours on our sofa. Then, quickly unzipping my slacks, I parted her petal-like nether lips and slid my cock inside her cunt. The flood of juices around my prick was overwhelming. I gripped her slim hips and slid back and forth inside her, once, twice, three times, before I could regain my balance, my decorum. Taking a deep breath, I spoke to her once again.

"I haven't finished with your spanking," I said sternly. "And I have a new rule for you to follow. Now, you must squeeze me with your pussy each time my hand meets your skin."

She knew to respond right away, saying, "Yes, Jack. I promise," so quickly that I sensed she was right on the verge of coming. Slipping my cock into her again, I resumed her spanking. First, I smacked the right cheek, then the left, and

Katie gripped and released my pulsing prick, just as I'd told her to. I sped up the rhythm, and she followed my lead, gripping into me with such seriousness that I felt as if I were being milked. What a fantastic sensation, my hand creating that warm, happy sound of applause on her naked skin while my cock was being treated to a series of decadent spasms from her dripping pussy.

How long would I be able to play the stern disciplinarian? Not much longer.

As Katie gripped and released me, I spanked her harder, faster, and soon we were coming together, no longer able to stave it off, to withhold ourselves from the finish line. But I did manage to speak just after I came, pulling out of her, then lifting her into my arms and sealing her to my body. I pressed my lips against her ear and whispered, "Katie, that was only round one."

She sighed in response and leaned her head back against my chest. "I know, Jack," she murmured. "Because I've been such an awfully bad girl."

One on One

SELENA DRAKE

You're opposite me on the couch, and it turns me on more than I could have imagined. It turns me on because you're watching me.

I'm wearing that short little dress, the one you like so much. One leg is up on the back of the couch; the other is on the floor. I'm not wearing any panties, and my hand is underneath, between my spread legs.

I'm slowly stroking my pussy. I'm very, very wet, just from having you watch me. My toys are laid out on the coffee table next to me: Every now and then, I see your eyes flicker to them with anticipation, with excitement. I can't believe I'm being such a dirty girl, letting you watch me. I can't believe it, but I love it.

I pull the skirt up higher, tucking it so that my pussy remains fully exposed. I don't think you noticed until now that

I shaved for you. You look a little surprised, and that turns me on even more. Did you think I wouldn't remember that conversation we had a while back about how sexy a shaved pussy is to you? And it seemed like the perfect time, since I wanted to make sure you could see *everything*.

I start with two fingers—usually I go for one at the beginning, but I'm much, much too turned on to settle for just one finger. Your eyes go wide as you watch them slide in. I'm moaning softly, squirming on the couch, my body moving in time with the throb of techno music from the stereo. I work my two fingers in and rub my clit with my thumb. My clit is hard, very hard, and it feels so good to stroke it. Watching you has me so turned on that I could probably come almost right away. But I don't want to come just yet; I want to savor your eyes on me as I do everything I do when I'm alone.

I take the vibrator, press the tennis-ball-sized head against my clit. I gasp as my pussy clenches around my fingers. My eyes go shut for a moment as I see stars; when I open them, I see you've got your cock in your hand, slowly stroking it as you watch me. It's as if we're in a peepshow booth, me putting on a show for you—and maybe you for me, too. That thought turns me on even more, and it makes me slip my fingers out of my pussy and reach for more toys.

I start with the narrowest of the three dildos. It slides inside me beautifully; I'm so wet that at first I don't even need any lube. I press the vibrator harder against my clit, arching my back as I gasp in pleasure. You're stroking faster, now, more and more turned on as you sense me getting closer. Within a few more strokes my pussy is starting to dry out a little, but that's OK—because I want more, much more. Holding eye contact with you as you stroke your cock, I reach out to the table again.

I ignore the middle-sized dildo and pick up the largest, putting the vibrator down across my lower belly just long enough to dribble lube onto the tip of the dildo. Then I slide the silicone cock inside me, and the thickness of the head feels so good inside me that I think, for a moment, that I'm going to come. But I don't; I just hover there, so close, as I watch your hand moving up and down on your hardness. God, I want you to come before I do. I don't know why; I just want to see your cock spurt, hear your moans of pleasure before I let myself go. I want to come knowing that my self-pleasure got you off, too, knowing that my fucking myself was enough to send you over the edge.

"Come for me," I say to you.

"Fuck your pussy," you sigh, and it's music to my ears. I begin working the thick dildo in and out of my pussy, holding the head of the vibrator firmly against my clit as I do. Your hand pumps furiously, and I recognize that sense of urgency that happens just before you come. I have to back off on the vibrator, taking it all the way off my clit, because you turn me on so much I think I'm going to come. But all of a sudden I know it's going to happen. The way your body twists, the way your hand tightens. And then you cry out, and come shoots out onto your hand.

The rush overwhelms me. I push the vibrator against my clit and move the dildo in and out of me rapidly, and I'm coming almost before you're finished. I thrash back and forth on the sofa, you coaxing me on with your moans of pleasure as you stroke your softening cock. My orgasm envelops me and I soar into it, my whole body alive with pleasure as our eyes meet.

My thighs come together, hard, and I have to turn off the vibrator or I'm going to start screaming. I relax into the sensations, feeling my pussy filled and my clit satisfied. I smile at you, as flirtatiously as I can manage, and I know I've fulfilled that fantasy you told me about. What I didn't expect is that you fulfilled mine.

And how convenient that is, since I'm planning to do it again. And again and again and again. One on one—just you and me.

Roger's Fault

ERIC WILLIAMS

It was Roger's fault that we were late.

"What a fucking day," he said, looking over at the piles of spreadsheets on my desk. "Let's go grab a beer."

I looked at my watch and shook my head.

"*One* beer," he insisted, and when I told him that I couldn't—when I said that you were at home, waiting—he asked, "What are you, man? Pussy-whipped?"

So, Christ, Elena—what was I going to do? One beer turned into two, turned into an hour-and-a-half of playing darts down near the pier at the Rose and Crown. By the time I realized how long we'd been playing, well, it was too fucking late to call and explain, anyway.

"We'll buy her something nice to make her feel better," Roger said, pushing me out the door to the parking lot. I shrugged uselessly. What could that possibly be? Flowers?

Candy? No way to buy back nearly two hours of lost time.

"Trust me," Roger said. "I know the perfect gift."

Then we were back in his shiny black pickup, cruising along Santa Monica Boulevard, through the sumptuous curves of Beverly Hills, cresting into Hollywood. I had my hand on my cell phone, trying to think up some excuse that didn't sound too lame, but he said, "It won't help to call now. We'll just show up with our gift and smooth things over."

Roger acted as if he really knew what he was talking about, and it sounded good, the way he said it. But when he pulled into the parking lot of The Pleasure Garden, I honestly thought he'd lost his mind.

"Come on," I smiled, shaking my head. "I'm not going into a vibrator store with you." Roger didn't even answer. It was obvious that he'd leave me in the truck if I didn't follow, so I kicked open the door and trailed after him. "You're crazy," I said, but he ignored my words, making me hurry to catch up, tripping down the steps and into the wonderful world of sex toys.

What a sight we made. Two guys in expensive work suits, perusing the aisles of marabou-trimmed nighties, edible panties, inflatable dolls, vibrators, paddles, lubricant. Roger acted casual about the whole thing, as if he shopped in stores like that every day. And then there was me, late as hell already, not knowing what the fuck we were doing there.

"Trust me," Roger said again, this time hefting a huge ribbed purple dildo and poking around in a basket for a suitable leather harness, one that would fit your slim hips without looking foolish. He wanted to find a quality-made harness with a delicate buckle. Not too large.

"You've got to be kidding," I said.

"Elena will love it. You'll see."

"You're not buying my girlfriend a dildo."

"You're right," he agreed, and I thought I saw sanity again in my buddy's green eyes. "I'm not buying it. *You* are."

"There's no way."

"Chet," he said, "you can't go home empty-handed. She's going to be upset as a wildcat that you're this late as it is."

"So, what?" I asked him, incredulous. "So I'm going to tell her to strap this thing on and fuck her aggression out on me?"

"Something like that."

And then suddenly, I understood. I'd been set up.

• • •

"She told you?" I asked, my voice cracking. I couldn't help but back away from him, standing against what I thought was a wall, but what turned out to be a display of artificial ladies, ready for a man to insert his cock in their mouths, asses, and pussies. Vinyl skin reached out to touch me, and I took a step forward, quickly, then whispered again, "She told you." This time, I wasn't asking.

"No problem with having a fantasy," Roger said, grinning now. He looked incredibly handsome with that knowing half-smile, his short dark hair, and a start of evening shadow on his strong jaw. "Especially when everyone gets off."

After that, he didn't say anything else. Simply grabbed the items he was looking for, snagged an extra-large bottle of lube from the display by the counter, and paid for his purchases. I have to admit, I had no idea what to do. First, there was the fact of my immediate erection, already making itself known against my leg. I felt as if I were back in high school, getting hard whenever the wind blew—or, more honestly, whenever the little cheerleaders danced onto the field for afternoon practice. Those tiny pleated skirts flipping up each time they cheered…what filthy mind created outfits like that?

And then there was the fact that my best buddy in the world knew that I wanted my girlfriend to ass-fuck me—and not only me, but to fuck him, as well. It had taken a lot of vodka before I'd confessed that particular kinky fantasy. Never thought the words would make their way to his ears.

Yes, Elena, I should have known, way back when we were sharing secrets. I ought to have guessed that you'd do something like this. Always ready to push the barriers in life, which is why I love you. But, thinking back, I realize that's why your brown eyes gleamed so brightly when I whispered the dirty words that made up my most private daydream. In your head, you were already playing this out: Roger and me, on our king-sized bed, and you, the queen of the night, going back and forth between us. Dipping into us. Taking us.

But still, I didn't think it would ever happen.

• • •

"Come on, Chet," Roger said, throwing one arm over my shoulder and herding me back to his truck as if he were leading a drunken man to shelter. "Elena's waiting."

At our house, the scene was carefully set. You weren't surprised that we were late, because it was all planned out from the start. The two of you know me too fucking well. Roger was sure he'd be able to coerce me into a game (or six) of darts. And you knew I'd feel so guilty that I wouldn't even have the balls to call. Ten minutes later, back at our house, there we were, Roger leaning hard on the doorbell before I could get my key out, and you, opening the door in your sleek leather pants, tight white tank top, high-heeled boots. You looked so fierce, I could have come on the spot.

"Boys," you said as a greeting. Just that word. Your eyes told me that I should have known better. That I was too slow to figure things out. Before I could respond in my own defense, we were walking after you like bad little kids heading toward the principal's office. Roger was the ringleader, taking my hand and pulling me down the hall to the bedroom, showing you the present he'd bought and actually undressing you and helping you put it on.

Fuck, Elena, the way you looked stripped down with that harness. Your pale skin, long dark hair, midnight eyes alert and shining. I wanted—well, you know damn well what I wanted. But I'll spell it out anyway. I wanted to go on my knees and get your cock all nice and wet with my mouth, to suck on it until the silicone dripped with my saliva, and then to watch as you fucked my best friend. I wanted to help glide the synthetic prick between the cheeks of his well-muscled ass, to watch you pump him hard, stay sealed into him, then pump in and out again. I couldn't wait to stand against the wall, one hand on my own pulsing cock, jerking, pulling, coming in a shower on the floor. Not caring what kind of mess I made, because, shit, I was beyond caring about anything like that.

That's not what happened, of course. We were in the wrong, coming back late like that. Me, especially, since I had a will of my own. I could have insisted that we go back to the house on time. Could have at least called. No, you wouldn't reward me by taking him first, letting me get off easy as the observer. That wasn't your plan.

"Naughty boy," you said. "Roger, help me bend him over."

At your words, there was a tightening in the pit of my stomach, like a fist around my belly. A cold metal taste filled my mouth, and it was suddenly difficult for me to swallow. Roger's seemingly experienced hands unbuckled my belt, pulled off my shoes, slipped my pants off, and took down my black satin boxers. Leaving those around my knees, he bent me over the bed, his exploring fingers trailing along the crack of my ass and making me moan involuntarily. Calloused fingertips just brushing my hole. Never felt anything that dirty, that decadent.

He was the one to help you. The assistant. Pouring the lube in a slick river between my ass cheeks, rubbing it in, his fingertips casually slipping inside of me. Probing and touching in such a personal manner that I could have cried. I wanted him to finger-fuck me, to use two, three, four fingers. I knew what it would be like to have his whole fucking fist inside of me. And, Elena, did I ever want that. Roger, behind me, getting the full motion of his arm into it. But then his strong hands spread me open as you guided the head of that mammoth, obscene purple cock into my asshole. And I wanted that even more.

Jesus-fucking-Christ, Elena. How did you know? I mean, I told you, of course, that night at the beach, draining the Absolut bottle between us as we stared up at the stars and out at the silver-lipped ocean. Your pussy so wet and slippery as you confessed your secret, five-star fantasy of fucking a guy. And me, harder than steel as I answered that it was what I wanted, as well.

But how did you know how to do it? How to talk like that? Sweet thing like you. Fucking me like a professional and talking like a sailor.

"Such a bad boy, needing to be ass-fucked," you told me, your voice a husky-sounding purr. "That's what you need—right, Chet? You need my cock deep in your hole."

That's what I needed, all right, and it was what you gave me. That dildo reaming my asshole, with Roger there, spreading my cheeks wide until it hurt. The right kind of hurt. Pain at being pulled, stretched open. Embarrassment flooding through me and making the pre-cum drip freely from my cock. I could feel the sweat on me, droplets beading on my forehead as I gripped into the pillow and held on. Never been fucked before, never taken, and here my best friend was watching. Helping.

As fantasies go, you never know what will happen when they come true. I turned to look in the mirror on the closet doors as Roger moved behind you, saw that your bare ass was plenty available since you were wearing only that harness. He wasn't rough with you the way you were with me. He knew how to do it, how you like it. On his knees behind you, parting your luscious cheeks and tickling your velvety hole with his tongue. Playing peek-a-boo games back there, driving the tip of it into your asshole and licking you inside out. Making you moan and tilt your head back, your hair falling away from your face, your cheeks flushed.

Then he was the one to pour lube all over his cock, to rub it in and part your heart-shaped cheeks and take you. I had a glimpse of his pole before it disappeared into your ass, and the length of it made me suck in my breath. What it must have done to you. Impaling you, possessing you as he took you on a ride.

The three of us fucked in a rhythm together like some deranged beast. You in my asshole and him in yours. Joined and sticky, reduced to animals that simply couldn't get enough. I didn't want to watch, but I had to, as the three of us came, bucking hard in a pile-up on the bed. Groaning, because it was so good. Better than good. It was sublime. Unreal.

But, in my defense, I have to say again that it was all Roger's fault.

Next Friday night, we'll be there on time, Elena. I promise.

Gerald

ALICE BLUE

She doesn't look like much. Still, when I look at the picture she gave me I get a quiet rush, a reverberation of what it was like.

I didn't feel anything like that when I knocked on her door that night, four years ago. It was routine, a noise complaint. I remember thinking, as I walked up the steps to the little house at 4467 Pierce Street, that anyone who blasted Beethoven couldn't be a lot of trouble to deal with. I was wrong.

She'd opened the door on the third knock. I sized her up the instant the door swung open: white Caucasian female, 35 to 37 years old, approximately 140 pounds, curly brown hair, green eyes, no obvious distinguishing markings. She'd been wearing jeans, tennis shoes, and a faded orange sweatshirt with the brooding face of her favorite composer on the front— whose 5th Symphony was now rattling the windows.

At the Academy they teach you never to make assumptions, that even the most innocent face can hide a nasty perp. "Treat every situation as a potentially dangerous one"—and if you do, you'll freak out in a matter of months. It had taken me a while, but I'd still managed to develop a set of cop instincts. The Academy would say to watch your ass, but my guts said that she was just some innocent little music fan.

As it turned out, the Academy was closer to the truth.

"Shit!" she'd said, with a comic intensity that made me smile despite myself. "Sorry, Officer." She dropped back into the place, moving quickly toward a wall-sized stereo setup, and Beethoven retreated to a percussive rumble. "Just got a little carried away, I guess. You know Ludwig: gets the old blood stirred up."

I can't remember what I said. I do remember, though, what I was staring at. You se a lot of shit when you're a cop—but in quiet little Bakersfield you don't see that much. I knew what I was looking at, of course. I'd seen more than my fair share in the magazines I kept hidden at home. Still, it was one thing to know something exists and quite another to see it personally.

I guess I must have stared for quite a while, because I was suddenly aware that she was looking at me. Shaking it off, I glanced at her and met a sly smile and those sparkling green eyes.

I didn't say a word as she closed the door behind me.

• • •

My I.D. reads GERALD PARROW. I still hate Momma for that, a name no one—let alone a kid—should get stuck with. To everyone except the Sergeant it's Jerry—not Gert, and certainly not Gerald. Usually all it takes it a frown and a low growl to get it corrected.

I learned quick. The Academy taught me a lot of things that weren't on the curriculum. Such as that black officers like me will always get the shit work, especially in little burgs like Bakersfield, and that we're going to get damned little respect— from citizens and especially from other cops. Momma always said I was a fast learner, and that was a lesson I picked up extra quick. After my first two weeks I put aside Gerald and built up Jerry: a tightly wound, no-nonsense, ball-breaking asshole. Of course, being a little over six foot helps, as does carrying 160 in firm muscles—wasn't always that way, as I had to build Jerry up in more ways than just attitude.

I was strong, I was mean, I was no one that anybody messed with, not even my "fellow officers." I was also real lonely.

I attracted some men, of course, and even some women, but you could see in their eyes that they wanted Jerry and not the whole package, Jerry but also Gerald.

Until that day she played Beethoven too loud—and I saw the whip.

• • •

I didn't ask, "Is it real?" as she got me a drink from the kitchen. I didn't need to; it had a very...lived-in look. Black leather strips, about a dozen or so strands. It looked heavy, it looked mean, it looked...I felt myself get hard just looking at it.

Her name was—is—Juliet. You wouldn't know it to look at her, old sweatshirt and running shoes, but she'd been doing this kind of thing for a while—not immediately obvious, but definitely noticeable as she spoke: "So, you want to play?" It wasn't so much a question as a mocking observation.

All I could do was nod as I sipped my drink.

"Then let's," she said, smiling broadly, eyes dancing. "Or would this be assaulting a police officer?"

I smiled back, reached up and plucked my badge from my uniform. Jerry was determined, Gerald was hungry.

She started with a kiss—not a polite peck on the cheek, but rather a forceful, hot stab with her tongue. Grabbing the back of my head, entwining her fingers in my curls, she jerked me back, hard. Gasping for air, I instead found her firm, soft lips, and strong, passionate tongue. Down deep, I felt myself respond on a very primal level.

"You're mine, Slut," she said with a bass growl. "For the next hour you are mine—a possession, an object, a thing. You exist for one, and only one, thing: to pleasure me. Do you understand me, Slut?"

I agreed. I tried to make it sound like "YESSIR!" but I'm afraid it was just little Gerald by then, Jerry having stepped out with that first hard kiss, and instead it came out "Yes...sir...."

"Now strip—show me what you've got," she said, pulling up a battered chair and sitting down, facing me.

Those men, and those few women, they'd wanted me to say those words, to growl commands, orders—but all that time, I wanted to hear them, too; to put aside the badge, gun, the attitude. To put aside Jerry.

I stood, slowly because my knees were weak, and started to unbutton my uniform. I didn't intend to do it slowly, but my fingers were shaking. One button, two, three. Shirt off. Then my boots, comically hopping braced against a doorjamb, but she didn't laugh. No, she watched. Not stared, just watched, with a gleam in those green eyes like a falcon or a leopard. I didn't know if she was going to fuck me or consume me—and that made me all the harder.

Naked, I stood in front of her, my cock painfully hard. She smiled, cruelly, and got to her feet. She inspected me, looking at my firm chest, my dark nipples, my ass, my stomach, my neck, my face, into my eyes. "You'll do," she said after a while.

"Thank you, Sir," I said in a weak voice, the carpet swaying beneath my feet.

"As an object you must meet my needs—satisfy my every desire. Do you understand me, Slut?"

"Yes, Sir," I said, distinctly aware of my throbbing cock, its moistened slit, the tingling in my nipples.

Then she said it—and if I was wet with pre-come before, I practically dripped after. "Lick my cunt," she said, a growl in her words, steel in her tone.

She kicked off her shoes, pulled off her jeans. No underwear. Her cunt was shaved, nothing between her legs but soft, white skin. It was lovely, a very pretty cunt, but it wasn't just her cunt I was begging for. She was already wet, I could tell: a sweet, musky smell. I got even harder—not for the sight of her cunt, the coming taste of her on my lips, but rather the command, the order.

She pulled up that battered chair again and sat down, spreading her legs. I'd licked more than my share of women—I'm not one of those brothers who sees licking pussy as something weak, not hardly. I'd done others, probably will do others—but this was my Master's cunt, the cunt I'd been ordered to lick, and so nothing could compare to it. Single-mindedly, becoming just an ecstatic licking machine, I worked on her—her slight moans and groans a glorious kind of applause for my technique, me wanting more than anything to please her.

I guess I got a little too enthusiastic, what with the joy at being pushed down, at being released from the bonds of my dominant Jerry, and I went a little too far. Her small yelp was like glass shattering, as if a part of my ideal world—the world of Gerald the lapping slave—broke, fell apart.

"Bad," she said, pushing me away and standing up, "very bad. Obviously you're in need of some training—because a real slave, an ideal slut, would never ever allow his teeth to even graze the cunt of his Master."

Jerry was frightened of nothing, but Gerald—little slutty Gerald—was terrified. "I'm so sorry, Sir," I pleaded in a soft little voice, bowing down toward her bare feet. "Please, I didn't mean to...."

I couldn't see her face, but I could hear the sneer in her voice. "Begging is so pathetic, even for a slut. Obviously you're in need of some severe discipline."

That was it. Right then I knew what was coming next. The magazines I'd bought, with their lurid fleshtones and shocking titles, had prepared me some—but not enough. They'd shown me the position: on my hands and knees, head down on the old carpeting, ass high in the air, legs slightly spread to bare my ass—but they had never gotten me ready for the first impact of the whip.

I expected pain—but it was more than that. At first it was a gentle slap, a glancing blow across both my cheeks. *That's it?* I remember thinking, almost frowning into the carpet, but then there came the next blow—harder, faster—and I knew that wasn't it. Oh, no, that wasn't it at all....

The impacts came faster, a pounding rhythm that may have started on my ass but soon became a drumming tremor through my whole body. It was as if my entire being was being beaten with a regular 4-4 beat, a drum in her sensual, masterful concerto.

My ass warmed, becoming almost hot, and my cock felt like it would explode—straining further with each thud of the whip. Each beat was like a great wave rolling through my body, starting at my ass and rippling through my belly, deep into my guts, thrilling my nipples and then out my mouth. At first I thought the sound was from somewhere else; it wasn't until later that I realized that I'd groaned with each impact, an echoing, deep rumble to her regular beating.

Jerry was nowhere to be found: It was just the slut, Gerald, receiving his exquisite punishment—and it was wonderful.

She said something, and it stopped, the cessation almost as shocking as the first impact. Distantly, I was aware that she reached down and helped me up, led me like a sleepy child.

My ass hitting the ground was less a shock than I expected, but I'd swear I could feel every whorl in the hardwood floor through the throbbing heat of my ass. With the whipping stopped, my body felt like it was going to deflate, sag from release—but then she produced a tiny plastic box. Inside: clothespins.

"Don't relax yet, Slut," she said, somehow grinning sweetly and nastily at the same time. "Your punishment isn't over—yet."

They were innocent looking. Just cheap, simple, wooden clothespins. No metal teeth, no vicious spring—nothing like in those magazines I'd seen. I almost laughed at them, thinking of Momma's clothesline, but then she put the first one on my right nipple.

My entire chest locked up in pain. I felt like a band had suddenly been wrapped around my chest, squeezed tight. I breathed carefully, slowly, to try and work through the pain. Somehow, without being aware of it, I'd shut my eyes. Realizing that, I opened them—and was staring right into her eyes: attentive, careful, concerned. Despite the pain, I nodded, realizing that I could take more.

And I did: one on my left nipple, then another one on the right side of my chest, then another one on the left side: four, five, six, seven—at eight I thought my teeth were going to break from the tension, my heart to stop from the pain wrapped around my chest, twisting my nipples. Again, my eyes were closed—so, again, I opened them: Her eyes were bright, excited. I knew that, despite the pain, she was here for me, she was my Master—and I smiled.

"I think that's enough," she said, and the first one came off—and I thought, then and there, I was going to die. Going on was bad, but coming off was murder. I thought for a second about screaming in pain, but then didn't want someone showing up for *that* noise complaint and finding me buck naked with this white woman and clothespins on my nipples. Despite the agony I smiled—until the rest of them came off.

My breathing was ragged and all I could do was moan and then moan some more—but slowly, eventually, the pain subsided, trailing off to a dull glow around my chest. I must have sat there for a long time, just breathing in and out, letting my body grow hotter and hotter with the pain and, yeah, the pleasure of what she'd done to me. Then, distantly, I was aware that she was getting me to my feet, leading me back, deeper into her apartment.

Though a bit blurry, I was still able to look at the room: noticed the great bookshelf of dusty, dog-eared volumes, the rack of CDs, the small pile of dirty laundry…and the brass bed. But as she led me in, I didn't see anything but her hand around my wrist—then the bed itself, vast and comforting.

"You have pleased me, Slut," she said, as if from a long distance. "You have pleased me with your performance—but there's one last thing I require."

I knew what was coming next, as if a deep part of Gerald was following some passionate script: I crashed down on my back on the bed, my cock throbbing, arms outstretched to grip the cool metal top corners of the brass bed.

Carefully, she crawled up on top of me, taking a brief second to kiss me on the lips before reaching back between her legs to ease my hard cock into her hot cunt. She started to fuck me—and again, like with the whipping, time vanished and I became her object, her slut. I lived for her pleasure, existed to service her: It was wonderful.

We fucked that first time for what felt like hours, her strokes rocketing through me as the whip had, but this time the impacts echoed through my body, not just from my reddened ass. Slowly, she pushed me higher and higher, up a slope I'd never been up before.

Then it happened—and shortly thereafter for her as well. The ecstasy was like a brilliant light in my eyes, a body rush, and a dreamlike collapse onto the soft comforter, onto her brass bed.

That was the first—there were many times after. Officer Jerry may have knocked on her door that first time, but it was slutty little Gerald who returned time and time again.

Check Your Inhibitions at the Door

ANN BLAKELY

Hunter has been to parties like this before. I can tell simply from the way that he's smiling at me. His light-gray eyes crinkle at the corners as he gives me what I've come to consider his "cologne model" expression. It's the gaze you always see in advertisements for men's fragrance. A slightly weathered-looking model, handsome, with a knowledgeable glimmer in his eyes, grins boldly from the pages of some fashion magazine. But Hunter isn't in a magazine. He is standing on the front step of Mica Malone's house, holding my hand reassuringly and waiting for me to ask questions.

I don't know where to start.

From inside the pocket of his worn leather jacket, he pulls out the invitation, casually handing it over for me to read. Even though I hold the card carefully, it shakes in my trembling grip. On the front of the invite is a closed door with golden light shining through a keyhole. Inside the card is written: "Check your inhibitions at the door." Aside from the time, the place, and the RSVP information, that's all it says. No explanation of fashion criteria. No helpful hints on how to behave. Maybe the rest of the guests know what to do at festivities such as this, but I have no idea. I've never been to a sex party before. At least, not outside of daydreams.

As usual, Hunter is charmed by my naïveté. "What would you like to know?" he murmurs before knocking. There are too many questions. And it's too late to ask, as our hostess suddenly appears, her image wavery, though still gazelle-like, through the smoked-glass panel. She opens the front door and beams out at us, all blonde upsweep and gleaming blue eyes.

"Kids," she says, welcoming us in her heavy, breathy voice. "Were you going to stand out there all night?"

Before either Hunter or I can speak, she ushers us indoors with a flurry of graceful gestures, quickly taking Hunter's coat and holding out one delicate hand for my red silk wrap. That's the way Mica is. She never waits for an answer. Still, this time is different. Maybe she understands my insecurities—read "terror"—and simply wants to pull me within before I lose my nerve and have to flee.

As she hangs our outerwear on an antique wooden coat rack, I frantically wonder where the rack is for our inhibitions. How will I ever manage to check mine at the door? Then I catch a glimpse of a large, sumptuous room at the end of the hallway, and—surprise, surprise—it looks just like a regular party. Colorful twisted candles stand on all the surfaces, creating a warm, inviting glow. People are mingling, drinking, laughing. I see lovely, multihued dresses on the women, simple dark suits on the men. Perhaps I was wrong to be so scared.

Another thought blooms in my mind. Maybe Hunter was teasing me. When he called at the last minute to invite me to a party, he explained that it was a kinky, free-for-all type of event where people played games they don't teach you in grammar school. But though he sounded casual, he knows that this is my number one sexual desire. Whenever we've engaged in that confessing game, whispering to each other late at night under the covers about what fantasy most turns us on, this is what I tell him: "I want to be seen."

"Describe it."

"I want to make love to you while other people watch." A hesitation. A breath. "While other people join in."

"You'd share me?"

"For a night—" I say. "One night only."

It's an image I've owned in my head for years, the concept of being on display for the pleasure of others. The idea of watching while another woman touches my man. Joins us. Helps us. But I am much too shy of a girl to have ever turned this fantasy into reality.

Too shy, that is, until tonight.

When Hunter told me that he knew where we could play like this, I thought he was kidding. Smiling, he teased me. "Are you up for it, Dara? Are you?" Hunter's a joker, though. I've always known that about him. So maybe this isn't *that* sort of party after all, I decide. Maybe he was simply testing me to see whether I'd truly be up for some similar event in the future. Ah, but why the sudden feeling of let-down within me? Where is the expected wave of relief?

Before I can psychoanalyze myself any further, Mica motions for us to follow her down the hall. "They're here, the stragglers," she announces in a voice rich with humor. "Let the games begin." Hunter and I trail behind her, and we are standing in the doorway watching as Mica glides easily to the very center of the room. The conversation stops as if on cue and all the guests turn to watch her.

Something is going to happen—something exciting. I sense it in the same way I can tell a rainstorm is approaching by the charge of electricity in the air. My heart races, and Hunter tugs on my hand, pulling me so that I'm standing directly in front of him and I can feel the delicious promise of his sudden hard-on pressing against my ass through my silky dress.

Oh, yes, I find myself thinking. *This is that sort of party.*

Hunter wasn't kidding, wasn't playing around. I wonder how I could have questioned the man who likes to talk dirty to me on his cell phone from the most public places. "I want to fuck you out on the balcony," he'll say while in line at a grocery store. "Be ready for me when I get home, baby. Be naked and ready." How could I have doubted a lover who always takes my worn pair of panties away with him in his pocket when he leaves me? A man who has gone down on me when our car was stopped in rush hour traffic, just trying to see how far he could get me to go before my nerves took over. Before I flushed a deep scarlet and insisted we waited until we could find a more private setting.

Now things are different, and I find myself thrilled at the prospect of being a part of whatever is about to take place. Magic accompanies a fantasy on the verge of coming true. This intense sensation works not only to thrill me, but to calm me. I feel as if I am being given an extravagant present, and I find myself so excited that when Hunter reaches one hand around and places his palm against the front of my dress, his fingers splayed to gently touch my pussy through the silk, I don't move his hand away.

The room hums with sexual promise. I can almost hear people's heartbeats resounding around me like exotic drums. When I glance quickly at the other guests, I see the rose-colored flush in the women's cheeks, the lustful heat reflected in the men's eyes. Our hostess is surrounded by a bevy of beautiful people, and I am grateful to be part of the crowd.

Then Mica takes off her panties, instantly setting the atmosphere for the rest of the evening. Yet, because she's Mica Malone, former fashion model and hostess extraordinaire, she doesn't simply take them off. There is art in her movements, theater in every gesture. This evening, she is clad in a floor-length shiny gray dress. More slip than dress, now that I look at it carefully, a piece of carefully crafted lingerie, made to look like outerwear until the sheer, fine lace panel at the top is noticed. Too fine to be worn outdoors. Meant only for the boudoir, or for naughty parties such as this.

With finesse, she hikes the creamy fabric up to her tiny waist and lets us all have a good long look at her lean, toned thighs. Only when she is absolutely certain that our attention is at the tightest possible level does she slip her manicured fingertips beneath the waistband of her all-lace panties and drag them down her legs.

We lean forward, as if one being, as if to hear the sound that gossamer-light fabric makes on skin. It is no sound at all, but I imagine the noise to be like the faintest whisper of music caught through an open window on a hot summer day.

At this moment, something even stranger happens to me. I have an inexplicably uncontrollable urge to go forward, part the circle of people, and help her step out of the under-garments. But I am apparently not the only guest who wants to help. A pretty, raven-haired girl wearing a short, sapphire-blue nightie-style dress beats me to the prize, moving quickly for-ward, then dropping in front of Mica and reaching for the panties. Mica is gracious as she bestows them on the lovely guest. Then, turning, she raises her arms over her head, and whispers, "Who will help with this?"

Now, I feel Hunter's hands on me, pushing me forward, as if he has read my desires and knows that I am desperate to be the one chosen. A true and gracious hostess to the end, Mica obviously senses my need as well.

"Dara," she says, turning my name not only into a state-ment, but into a command. I make my way forward, and it feels as if I am in a waking dream as I bring my hands to Mica's slender waist and lift, lift, lift her filmy slip over her head. As I do, she sighs and closes her eyes, and it is gratifying to be responsible for a little bit of her pleasure.

But now Mica is naked, and the rest of us are behind her in the games. We can't let her win so soon, can we? From the corner of my eye, I see the partyers quickly catching up. Men peel off their suit jackets, hurry to lose the shirts, slacks, boxers or briefs. Women, with less to remove, assist each other with any hard-to-reach buttons and zippers, tugging, pulling until I sense that I am surrounded by nude guests and that I am the only one left clothed.

The only one, but for Hunter.

He comes forward now, joining me in the center of the room. Slowly, he puts his hands on my shoulders and turns me so that I am facing him. He kisses me once, long and slow, his tongue meeting mine and further igniting my sense of dangerous desire. When we part, his eyes tell me secrets, make me promises. Deep within them, they ask me questions. *Is this OK? Am I all right? Do I want to stop?*

I answer with actions rather than words. Putting my arms over my head, I close my own eyes and let him undress me. To the chorus of soft moans that surround us, Hunter undoes the ties at the top of my dress and slides the crimson satin sheath over my head. Beneath I have nothing on, and this makes him hesitate. He understands that I chose not to wear panties as a way of shocking him. And I have managed to do just that. Do I win? Am I now in charge of surprising him?

When I open my eyes again, he is smiling at me in a brand-new way. The expression remains on his face as he removes his own clothes, and I warm at the sight of his fine, muscular body. It is a body I have admired many times before, but now is different. Now he is on display not only for me, but for the masses. Then I feel Mica's fingers on my shoulder blades from behind, and the three of us move to a gold-covered velvet chaise longue that seems to have been perfectly positioned for our pleasure.

"You're OK with this?" Hunter asks me softly once we reach our destination, his lips warm against the skin of my neck, his arms around my waist. I nod, fascinated by the activities around us, but Hunter wants more information from me. "You understand what I'm asking?"

Now I turn and look into his sterling-gray eyes, and I realize that he wants a verbal response. Am I willing to turn our solid twosome into a temporary threesome? Will it change what we have? I know that answer instantly: undoubtedly, yes. But will it change us for the better, or for the worse? I have a split second to deal with all the standard feelings of jealousy, of insecurity, of fear that any normal woman would possess at the concept of watching her boyfriend make love to another. Hunter is waiting for my answer, and I realize that if I want to leave, he will take my hand and lead me away.

Around the room, groups of guests have found each other and entwined themselves in new and unusual positions. I get different images each time I move my head. Flickers of fantasies come to life as I see women going down on women while men help by holding open slippery pussy lips or slicking back a partner's hair. People interlock like sexual puzzle pieces, and I find myself getting even more turned on as I see the raven-haired girl who took off Mica's panties sliding back into them herself. She sprawls out on the floor, and a well-built young man begins to eat her through the expensive lace.

When I turn back to our little trio, I know that I can't leave now. I have waited forever to play like this. To be in a safe situation where I can do exactly what it said on that invitation: Check my inhibitions at the door. Yes, I feel a pang when I see Mica place her hand on Hunter's inner thigh. But that pang is quickly replaced by a different, more urgent sensation. One of lust, both hungry and demanding. And perhaps the emotions of jealousy, of insecurity, are what raise my excitement to a previously unreached height.

"We stay," I tell my boyfriend. "Please, let's stay."

Hunter kisses me again, and then we create our own new positions on the chaise longue. At my words, Mica is the one to smile and make the first move, to sink to her knees and part her full lips around Hunter's cock. He is in instant ecstasy, sighing and running his hands through Mica's long blonde hair, now down from its carefully constructed upsweep, but I feel slightly unsure of what to do. Should I just watch, becoming once again an audience member as I am in most of my dealings in life?

Before I can decide, Mica bobs her head off Hunter and instructs me, "You lick his balls while I do this." It's as if she understands that I need instruction, and that sense of peace I felt earlier returns to me again. Because this is something I can definitely do. I move to join Mica at her side, and Hunter seems deliriously happy at the prospect of having two women playing him simultaneously. "Oh, my girls," he moans as Mica sucks his cock and I get between his legs and begin to lick and kiss his balls. "My lovely girls."

In the candlelight, the room takes on a hedonistic aura, as if our little trio has been transported back in time to Roman orgies, where decadence was not only encouraged but rewarded. But after a few minutes of being treated to such fabulous sucking, Hunter wants more action. He moves up on the sofa and, with a look divided evenly between me and Mica, he gets behind her. As he slips his cock between her thighs, he murmurs to her, "Go down on Dara while I fuck you. I want to watch her face change as you make her come."

Mica motions for me to move closer, and as Hunter thrusts inside her, she gives me my first tongue-lapping ever from a woman. She senses just what I want, even before I truly know myself. With a powerful movement, she slides two fingers into my sticky pussy and then begins to tease my clit with her lips. She works slowly and gently, giving me just the right amount of tension when she locks her lips around my pearl and begins to suck.

As Hunter drives into her, Mica starts to moan, and the noises she makes reverberate within me. We are in rhythm together, the three of us in perfect synch, Hunter choosing our course and keeping us steadily moving forward. I open my eyes to see him looking down at me, and he tilts his head and then whispers for me to watch. I obey, staring as he blows out a nearby candle, wets the larger end with his mouth, and then parts Mica's heart-shaped rear cheeks with his free hand. I know what is going to happen before Mica is aware of it. Hunter slides the spit-lubed candle end inside her, and Mica suddenly makes even more desperate, mewing noises against my cunt.

Watching her get filled in two holes makes me climax, creaming against Mica's mouth as Hunter leans forward and grabs hold of me. The electricity between the three of us is connected in a circle of flesh, and as I come, and Hunter comes, Mica climaxes between us.

It is an awakening for me. Pure and simple. And in a hazy, dreamy way, I recall the image on the cover of the invitation. In my mind, that closed door swings open and an unimaginable range of pleasures floods free.

Roaming Charges

CHARLOTTE POPE

I had been planning it for weeks, had even had several false starts. Not because I was afraid—hell, I wasn't the one about to be embarrassed in public—but because I wanted to do it early, before Aaron had gotten used to the little wearable cell phone he'd bought. If I did it to him while the device was still a novelty, I figured he'd be less surprised, less shocked…and it would be a hell of a lot less exciting. That's why I waited a full three weeks.

I had given him endless shit about the device, just as I had when he'd bought his first cellular phone. I'd teasingly called him a yuppie, a sell-out; told him he wasn't punk rock anymore. As if I hadn't noticed that neither of us had been particularly punk rock for about five years—but never mind about that. I thought the idea of wearing your cell phone on your face like some bastard spawn of Madonna's microphone was the most ridiculous thing I'd ever heard of. You can see these things anytime you walk around the financial district—it's probably the same in any big city, really. They're these little headsets that attach to a device that you keep in your pocket, allowing you to make phone calls with your hands free—or, more to the point, to walk the streets appearing to talk to yourself like a maniac. I razzed Aaron mercilessly about it.

It was fun to tease him, but I think I hurt his feelings a little bit. Which is why I felt doubly compelled to give him *and* his phone a little make-up gift to show that there were no hard feelings.

Then again, maybe it was just being "between jobs" that gave me such filthy ideas. Sitting around on the couch naked all day, savoring the knowledge of all that severance pay in our bank account. That, not to mention refraining from showering and eating half a pint of Ben & Jerry's for lunch, all have a way of working positively surreal magic on your libido, I've found.

And it could have just been the automatic association—the last time I'd spent any length of time at home had been right after college. Then, I'd been home because I was doing phone sex, sometimes as many as twenty calls a day. Being home all day, I couldn't help but remember those times with fondness. And maybe I just couldn't control myself.

I knew Aaron would leave the office right at five; he always did on Fridays. Besides, we had theater tickets, so he'd want to get en route as fast as possible, even though the play wasn't until eight. I knew I could count on his being right where I wanted him.

I undressed, put on my garter belt and stockings, the white ones, my little white silk robe—no bra. I even put on my white spike heels, because Aaron was so partial to them. I sat down in the big easy chair, though; no way am I standing around in spike heels for *anyone*.

I put on my favorite Dance Thrust CD—throbbing, thumping industrial-house, loud enough to give me some rhythm but not so loud as to drown out what I knew would be the delicious sounds of Aaron squirming.

I waited until the clock said 5:14, then I called him.

"Hello?"

"You're on the bus."

"I decided to take the train, actually."

"Ooooh, even better. Trains are long and thick, and they go fast through tight little holes deeeeeep in the ground. You know what I'm wearing?"

"Excuse me?" Aaron's voice sounded nervous.

I cuddled up in the chair, letting my robe fall open, feeling the hot summer air on my bare thighs, belly, breasts.

"I asked you if you knew what I was wearing. I'll give you a hint: not much."

"That's…uh…very interesting." Now he sounded *really* nervous. "What's that music?"

"Dance Thrust," I said. " 'Bound to the Throb.' My very favorite disk to fuck to. Remember when you fucked me to this last week?"

"I remember," said Aaron, obviously trying to sound casual and conversational.

"Every time I hear this music I want to touch myself. I'm

touching myself now. I'm playing with my clit. This music makes my clit throb. Is it crowded on the train?"

"Very crowded, actually," he said. "Standing room only."

I giggled gleefully, pulled my robe further open to reveal my breasts. "Oh, so if you were to get, say, a big raging hard-on, everyone would be able to see?"

"Uh…yes," he said. "Definitely."

"Well, then, it probably wouldn't be very nice for me to tell you that I've got my big black dick sitting out on the coffee table, just waiting for me to shove it inside me. And I'm thinking about how it could be *your* dick."

I began to play with myself in earnest.

"That's…um…very interesting."

"Now I'm rubbing my pussy. I didn't realize how wet it was. I could just shove that dick right in there. I wouldn't need any lube. It's the big one."

"The bigger of the two," he said flatly.

"Careful! You don't want the people around you to know you're having phone sex with your wife! Or can they already see your big hard-on?"

"Not sure about that," he said tersely.

"But you *are* hard."

"That's affirmative."

"Then they can probably see you. Don't you let any of those bus-riding whores start sucking your dick, understand?"

"Oh, no," he said. "I don't think that's a danger."

"Well, if you're standing up, your dick's probably at face level, right?"

"Kind of," he said.

"Gooood. Just imagine it's me in that seat in front of you. I'd start sucking you off, no matter how many people were watching. Would you like that?"

"Not sure it'd be appropriate," said Aaron uncomfortably. "But yes."

I giggled. "Come on, I know what an exhibitionist you are. You'd love it. I'd love it, too. I'd take your dick out of your suit pants and run my mouth all the way up it to the head…you think you're leaking some pre-cum?"

"Not sure," said Aaron.

"Leaking a little pre-cum for your girl? Think I could lick it off?"

"Probably."

"Oh, I think you are. I'd suck it right off the head of your cock. Lick it off, run my tongue all over you. Would that feel good?"

"Yes," he said.

"Think I would look good doing it?"

"No doubt."

"Want me to tell you what I'm wearing?"

"Yes."

"Well, not yet. Why don't you just make some guesses in your mind while I slip my fingers inside me…oooooooh." I eased two fingers into my pussy and found it slick with desire. I pressed them in easily, as deep as they would go, and began to pump my fingers into my pussy while rubbing my clit with my thumb. I was really close to a climax already—whether from the forced exhibitionism or just the pleasure of talking dirty after so many hours of technical terms, I couldn't begin to speculate.

"My pussy's so wet…I'm dripping on your favorite chair. You know it smells like you?"

"Is that a fact?"

"Now it's going to smell like me. Like my pussy. I'm incredibly wet. I think I could put this big black dick inside me without any lube. Would that be hot?"

Aaron always found it incredibly exciting when I was able to get a dildo inside me without lube. Didn't happen often, but I was plenty wet enough now.

"Want to take a guess about what I'm wearing?"

"No," said Aaron.

"All right…after I was done licking the pre-cum off your cock, then I'd take you in my mouth, all the way down. I'd pump your cock into my mouth, down my throat. And start sucking you off. I'd suck your cock until you shot in my mouth."

"Really. Is that right?"

"Am I making you uncomfortable?"

"You most certainly are," Aaron said.

I smiled. Maybe I was a bit of a sadist but, knowing how uncomfortable this made him, I responded, "You could always hang up, then."

"No," he said. "I couldn't."

"Oh, good," I said. "You're so hooked you *can't* hang up."

"Something like that."

"Is your dick nice and hard?"

"Uh-huh."

"What I'm wearing," I told him as I reached out for the big black rubber dildo—my favorite cock to fuck myself with, after Aaron's—"is that new garter belt I wore the other night."

"The white one?"

"That's right, the white one. With white seamed stockings, and my white robe."

"The little one."

"Yes, the little one," I said, sliding the dick up between my legs. I spread my thighs wide and nuzzled the head into my pussy. Normally I would have needed a few good spurts of lubricant, but I knew I was so wet from talking to Aaron—not to mention thinking about this scene all day long—that the dick would slide right in. "The tiny one that's practically see-through. And I'm not wearing a bra; you know how I am about my tits. The robe's rubbing my nipples. As if I wasn't horny enough. I'm going to fuck myself now."

With a loud groan, I pushed the head of the dildo into my pussy, feeling its snug fit, stretching me. I shuddered—I knew I was going to come any moment. I began rubbing my clit with one hand while I pumped the dildo in with the other.

"I just shoved it inside me," I said breathlessly. "All the way, as deep as it would go. God, it feels so good. Almost as good as having your cock inside me. Would that feel good?"

"I'm sure it would," said Aaron.

"God, it feels good on this end. I love having your cock inside me. But this'll have to do."

"I'll be home in a few minutes," said Aaron.

"I can't wait a few minutes!" I whined, fucking myself. "I'm going to come now! I'm fucking this big cock into my pussy...rubbing my clit...." I was having trouble speaking, my breath coming short. I lifted my ass off the chair so that I could fuck myself better. I pumped myself with one hand and rubbed my clit with the other—and then I reached that point where I knew it was coming, I knew it was going to happen....

"Oh, God," I moaned softly. "I'm coming! I'm coming right now!"

"Oh, yeah," said Aaron, unexpectedly, his voice low and husky. "That's so good. Fuck your pussy. Fuck it hard. Fuck yourself silly!"

Hearing him talk like that, knowing he was on the bus, knowing people could hear him talking dirty to me, see his big hard-on, drove me over the top. My orgasm washed over me and I spasmed, arched my back, screamed into the phone, hearing it crackle with static as my cries of pleasure rose. I was moaning and screaming so loud that I didn't realize until after I'd settled down into the chair, utterly spent and basking in the afterglow of my pleasure, that Aaron was standing in the doorway grinning at me, the front door open behind him.

"Wouldn't you know it?" he said. "The one day the bus is on time."

"Close that door," I rasped, my voice shot from screaming so loud. "Some of us are naked."

He slammed the apartment door. A shudder went through my body as he dropped his briefcase and came toward me, smiling and unfastening his pants.

I smiled back at him and hung up the phone. We were going to be late to the theater again.

Panties

BILL VICKERS

I'm getting out of the shower and Marie is drying me with the large, thick maroon towel. She's naked, too, but I tell her I'm late for work already, she'll have to wait until tonight, but she says she knows I have to go, she won't delay me again—although she's on her knees before me now and drying my legs and I'm getting excited again just looking at her, her mouth so close—but she says, "I just want you to think about me all day."

I will, I say.

"I want to be sure you think about me all day."

Believe me, I say, I can't forget this morning, or last night, or yesterday morning….

"You might."

Impossible, I assure her.

"But you'll be in meetings, you'll have to pay attention to

what people are saying, phone calls will come in, you'll be figuring estimates, you'll be drawing blueprints—"

I say I *do* need to finish the plans for the LeFarge house, that's true, but, I assure her, I will have her in my mind, at least in the back of my mind.

"I need to be sure," she says, "you'll be thinking of me."

Well, I say, suppose I call you every hour or so?

"And the other fifty-nine minutes?"

Really, I say, I think about you all the—

"I want you to wear my panties."

I'm looking down at her. She's still on her knees in front of me. You want me to—

"The emerald green high-cuts, with the lace. The ones you gave me for my birthday."

But, Marie—

"You'll be aware of them all day. It'll be as if I'm holding you down there"—she stands, cupping me down there—"and I'll feel as if I'm with you every moment. You won't forget me."

I say I could never forget her. But wear her panties? I'm a guy, I say. Guys don't wear women's underwear. Not normal guys. Do you want me to be one of those guys who likes to pretend he's a woman?

"It's only my panties," she says. "No one will know. No one but you. And me."

. . .

Well, I discover it's tricky taking a leak—no opening, you know, in her emerald green high-cuts with the lace. So I have to go into the stall and sit every time I have to pee, like a woman. Bob, my partner, notices after a while and asks if I have diarrhea. All I can do is say, Yes.

But the truth is, I think about Marie all day. I feel that silk hugging my balls and pressing my pecker, and I have to admit, it's exciting. I can't wait to get home.

When I get home, she's playing a little game. She's never done this sort of thing before, but I think, what the heck, she's adding more spice to our life, because as I walk in the door, she says, innocent as can be, "Ron, I can't find my high-cut emerald green panties with the lace. Are you wearing them?" And before I can answer—I don't know what to answer, in fact—she unbuckles my belt and unzips my pants and my pants drop to my ankles, and she says, "Oh, Ron, you *are* wearing my panties, you naughty boy." Then she pulls off my tie and unbuttons my shirt, and then she lifts her dress over her head, and she stands there, on her firm trim legs, her pink lips smiling, her pert breasts jutting, wearing only my blue cotton bikini shorts. "I thought of you all day, too."

She kisses me, her tongue probing my mouth. She squeezes my chest, as if I have breasts. She pinches my nipples. She sucks my nipples. "Ron," she says sadly, "your breasts aren't very big."

I don't know why it turns me on.

"That's OK," she says. "I like small-breasted girls."

I feel her breasts, squeeze their plumpness, pull at her pink nipples. I bend down to suck her nipple, but she raises my head. "I have something else in mind," she says. She leads me into the bedroom. She tells me to lie down.

"What's gotten into you?" I ask, smiling, still standing.

She smiles back, coquettish. Her palm pats my buttock. "It's what's going to get into *you*," she coos, and pushes me onto the bed.

I lie there, looking up at her. Her auburn hair is tousled, a little wild. Her face is flushed with excitement. She says, "Turn over."

I roll onto my stomach. Suddenly I feel strangely vulnerable.

"Don't move," she says.

I wait.

"I'm taking your shorts off," she says.

That's a start, I think. I hear a drawer open. Other sounds I can't identify. I peek over my shoulder. A nervous thrill shivers my body. She's strapping on a penis—black straps, pink penis, erect but pliable, about the size of mine, an average size.

She sees me watching.

"You peeked."

I watch her.

"You're a bad boy."

She reaches into the drawer. She pulls out a riding crop. I'm sure she's merely teasing.

The crop stings my buttock.

I don't say anything. This is a new sensation.

She smacks me again. Then nothing. Finally she says, "You look so defenseless like that, on your stomach. So exposed."

I don't say anything.

"Get on your knees, your ass in the air."

I do.

Something oozes into my crack. It must be the K-Y.

Her finger slips into my anus. She slides it in and out slowly, working it in circles. I keep my head down, look at the sheet. I like not seeing. I like being passive like this. It's a new sensation. How did she know I would like this? Or does she care? Maybe this is only for her. No, she knew I'd like it. Everything she does is for both of us—putting her hand in my pants at the movies, calling me at work and telling me how she's playing with herself, thinking of things I'd like even before I think of them, like the time she made a video of her friend Wanda masturbating and showed it to me.

I feel my anus stretching. She must have two fingers in. They circle, expanding me more. I feel strangely humbled, obedient.

"You have a tight ass, Ron," she says.

Make it bigger, I say.

She pushes in. She makes it bigger. Three fingers?

My cock lengthens and thickens.

"You're bad, Ron."

Her other hand smacks my ass.

"What's happening to your cock?"

She smacks again, harder.

"Are you playing with yourself?"

I shake my head.

"Go ahead," she says. "Feel your cock getting hard."

I lean on an elbow, stroke myself.

"Oh, Ron," she says. She smacks me again. I let go.

Her fingers leave. My anus feels suddenly abandoned. Yet I seem to still feel her fingers, a pressure remaining.

"You know, Ron, I have a cock, too."

My cock gets harder.

"My cock's getting hard, too," she says, her voice soft and enticing. I imagine her with a real cock. I imagine it getting hard, standing up.

I feel her hands on my buttocks.

"It's the size of your cock."

Her thumbs pull my cheeks apart.

"You'll feel what I feel when you fuck me."

I feel something nuzzle at my anus.

"You'll be me."

Something pushes in.

"I'll be you."

It slides in a couple of inches, easily, then stops. It's a good feeling, but it's not enough.

"That's as far as my fingers went," she says.

I feel her cock poised, stretching my anus.

"Do you want more?"

I want more, I say.

She slaps my buttocks. "Ron, you're so bad."

You make me bad, I say.

She plunges in. It hurts for a second, then it feels fine. It fills me. It doesn't move.

"Ron, your cock is hard."

Without thinking I wrap my hand around my cock.

She spanks me hard. "Naughty."

I let go.

Her cock slides slowly out. Will she leave me? I wait. Her hands are on my buttocks, still spreading my cheeks.

Marie? I say.

"What do you want, Ron?"

Put it in, Marie.

I feel it slide slowly in.

In farther, I beg.

She slides it in farther. Slowly, teasingly.

She nuzzles it around. She pulls part way out. She slides in. Out. In.

Marie is fucking me in the ass.

"Do you like it?" she asks.

Yes.

She fucks me harder.

Fuck me, Marie.

"I'm fucking you, Ron." She slaps my buttocks. "Is your cock hard?"

It's hard, Marie.

"Play with it, Ron."

But I don't.

"Jerk yourself off," Marie orders.

You do it, I say.

"You bitch," she says. "You know I like that, don't you?" And her hand slides over my hip, her fingers curl around my cock, her hand pumps my cock as her cock pumps in my ass. She goes faster, then slows down. She stops.

Don't stop, I say.

She starts again, slowly.

Faster, I say.

But she doesn't speed up. She tortures me. She hangs me on the brink.

"Are you going to come?" she asks. But she can tell, her hand slippery.

She pulls out of my ass. Is she quitting? No. She kneels beside me on the bed, her ass in the air. "Fuck me, Ron. Fuck my ass."

I stand behind her. Her ass is already lubricated. I spread her sweet, soft cheeks, so round, so plump. I tease her pink bumhole, so enticing, so inviting.

"Don't tease me, Ron."

Play with your cock, I say.

She grabs her cock.

I slide in easily.

She says, "Oh, God, that feels good."

I pump in and out. It feels good to me, too.

She says, "I wish I had a real cock, like yours."

So do I, I say.

"Really?"

Really, I say. I pump slowly.

"I wish you had a pussy," she says.

So do I, I say. I wish I had a pussy like yours.

"Fuck me harder, Ron. Fuck my ass."

I fuck her harder. She moans. I say, I can still feel you in my ass. It's like your cock is still there, still fucking me, while I'm fucking you.

She whimpers.

I reach around her hip. I grab her cock. I pump her cock the way she pumped mine.

"Yes, yes!" she whimpers. "It hits my clit when you do that."

I pump my cock into her ass as my hand jerks her cock

into her clit. I slide out as my hand slides out.

"Faster!" she says.

I slow down.

"Bitch!" she says.

I go slow.

"Please, Ron, please."

I go slower.

She shoves her ass at me, moves it faster. I hardly have to move. Her ass is fucking my cock. She moans in relief.

I'm rock-hard. I can't tease any longer. I speed up. I'm ready to come.

"Yes! Yes!" she cries.

I slip my finger under her cock. I feel her clit, hard and wet.

She presses her fingers on mine. We rub her clit together.

"Fuck me," she moans.

I'm fucking you, I gasp.

My whole body seems to orgasm, heels to cock to head.

I come in her ass.

"I feel it," she says.

I squirt and squirt. It seems as if it will never end.

"You're filling me up," she says.

Her fingers press mine, hold them to her throbbing clit. She stiffens. She cries out. She moans as if in exquisite pain.

We stay like that for several moments, as if frozen, my chest to her back, my cock in her ass, both our fingers on her pussy. Her juices drip into our hands.

I grab her breasts, hanging free, and squeeze. I smear her juices on them.

She licks my hands.

Finally I slide out of her ass. I pull her cheeks apart. I see my semen oozing from her hole. It drips down into her pussy.

I kneel behind her. I lick her asshole.

I fall on the bed beside her. She leans over me, her breasts rubbing my chest. She puts her lips on mine. I open my mouth. She sticks in her tongue.

"I taste you," she says. "I taste me."

We lie on our backs beside each other, catching our breaths, dripping with sweat, juices dripping between our legs.

The next morning I'm getting ready to dress for work. I open her lingerie drawer. I pull on her powder-blue bikinis. I reach for my trousers.

"There's something else today," she says.

Don't worry, I say. I'll think about you.

She hands me her white garter belt and her white stockings. "I know you will," she says. I look at her. She's put on a pants suit. There's a bulge in the crotch.

Please

ERIN PIPES

The fantasy has been brewing in the back of my good-girl mind since puberty—rolling through my brain like a movie, while I whimpered behind closed doors, one hand clamped firmly between my wet thighs. Since I left the clutches of my parents' home, and their spare-the-rod, spoil-the-child sensibilities, it has grown more demanding, nagging at me. I pushed and pushed and pushed at you to help me realize this, until finally you relented. Your timid slaps on my ass weren't enough to punish a wayward toddler. Nary a rosy-hued handprint in sight! Not to mention your tendency to cringe and ask if I'm all right after each blow, compassion I appreciate in every other circumstance. It was disastrous.

"I'll do anything for you," you said. "Could you be more specific about what you need?"

Since you asked....

You could be a father, brother, uncle, priest. Or nobody. Faceless, but older, rigid, stern, commanding. Male. Typically stereotypical.

You sit on the edge of a bed. Your sleeves are rolled up, cuffed at the elbow. I can see the veins pumping in your forearms. I am defiant and outfitted in Catholic schoolgirl cliché. My tanned calves strain against the regulation white kneesocks. The skirt is a little too short for your liking. My large, dark nipples peer through the sheer, white fabric of my shirt. I'm pouting, preening, younger than I look.

I start off by teasing you. I bend at the waist to rearrange my socks, showing off my ripe, bared ass. You are embarrassed —angered. I giggle, mocking you. I am such a bad girl, really.

You are still and your eyes are cold and staring. Suddenly, your hand flies at me, grabs my wrist, twisting it under. I wince. Show me your fingers, clamped tight and then tighter, turning red, then white with pressure. You will not be mocked. While you hold my wrist, your other hand passes through my hair, gently grazing my cheek. Slip two fingers between the buttons on my starched blouse and rip it open. Paw at my exposed breasts, full and lovely. Pinch my nipples fiercely and hold my gaze. Humiliate me with your rough touch. Leave your mark.

I will fight you, slap your hand away. Buck against the reins of your fist, clamped unrelentingly around my wrist. When I call you a fucking bully, you smile. When I cry out and plead with you to let go, you only tighten your grip. There are no safewords here. My hand goes numb. When I reel back and spit in your face, your smile turns sinister. I notice the stirring in the crotch of your trousers and feel a shudder up my spine.

The burden of being a strong woman falls to the floor with my torn blouse. In here, I am a little slut, and you tell me so. Your voice is so calm and smooth. Tears stream down my face as you list my sins: insolence, pride, promiscuity. You set me on your lap and let go of my wrist, hold my face in your hands, lick the salty trails off my cheeks. I'm so bad, you say, but you can absolve me. You don't say it will hurt you more than it hurts me. That's a lie I don't need or want to hear. It's *supposed* to hurt me, and I can trust that you'll make sure it will.

"Look at yourself," you command, while your eyes grope my naked breasts. When I obey, peering down over my body, you hurl me to the floor. The carpet burns the thin skin over my hipbone. I disgust you. Still, my spirit is unbroken. I arch my back hungrily, running my hands across my body. Holding your gaze, challenging you, I thrust one hand under my little skirt and two fingers slide in easily. I bring the shiny fingers to my lips, suck them into my mouth, savoring the salty cream. I lick them clean, and a moan escapes from the back of your throat. "You dirty bitch," you mutter so softly it's almost endearing. The first slap comes then, across my cheek and harder than I expected. My ears ring.

You pull me from the floor and across your lap. Face down. Your erection pushes against my aching clit, and I wriggle slightly, longing for the release of that pressure. You say, "Do you feel that, what you've done to me?" I'm lost in the pattern of the bedspread and the tingling of your hand smoothing under my skirt. You pull a bottle of lube from your shirt pocket, fingering my asshole. "Goddammit," you whisper as your middle finger slips in past the tightness of that hole.

My hands clutch the blankets and I draw a quick breath, grinding my hips against you, insistently. "Be *still*," your voice warns. It is agonizing, the way you draw it out, the way your hand forces my head into the mattress while you work your finger inside me.

"Has a man ever entered you here?" you ask. I pause, not knowing which truth you want.

"…No," I finally answer. My voice is strained and unrecognizable.

You pull your finger from me and your hand comes down hard on my ass in two quick smacks. The skin burns. "That was a *lie*," you tell me. "Do you actually expect me to believe this is a virgin asshole?" Your hand is moving in slow circles. My pussy throbs so hard, I know you can feel the vibration. The seam of your trousers pulses against me, and I press my hips into you again.

"I told you to be still," you say, and there are two more sharp smacks on my ass. Harder than before. My teeth bite down into my lip as I try, unsuccessfully, to stifle a longing moan.

"Oh, you like that? You *dirty* girl," you say, smiling wickedly. Your hand comes down again, slaps that make your cock buck into me. I spread my legs to receive the fullness of your hand, press my hips into you with each stinging smack. I cry out from the pain. I'm almost coming and you sense this. One step ahead. The slapping stops abruptly, and you are tolerant again with your soothing circles. I feel the heat rising from my skin; your hand is strangely cool.

"You've gotten my good slacks wet with your juices," you scold, reaching down to feel the moist spot on the fabric, tracing it to the swollen lips of my cunt. Your fingers slide into this moisture, then quickly out again. I taste blood from where I've bitten my lip. "I need to get these out of the way," you remark, fumbling one-handed with the button on your waistband. "You'll probably leave a stain." I think of your thick, naked cock sliding into me, anywhere, and a whine escapes my lips. I hear the descent of your zipper and almost turn my head to catch a glimpse, but the rules are clear. I'm not to look, to move, without your permission. I want your strong hand coming down on my raw flesh—I will do anything to incite you, but the game has changed. My desire is as plain as the creamy wetness I've left on your trousers. You know not to give it to me. For now....

"Stand up," you command. I move off your lap reluctantly. You rise from the bed and your trousers fall to the floor. Your cock stands rigid and angled from your body, twitching. Menacing. The drop of moisture on the tip makes my mouth water. You catch me staring and ask, "Do you want to suck it, Sweetheart?" Your voice is gentle again. I smile up at you, beaming. *Oh, yes, Daddy. Please.* It is all the coaxing I need, to fall to my knees in front of you. I run my hands up and down the velvety skin of your penis, mesmerized. I want the approval of your load shooting down my throat. My mouth swells with slickness, like a cunt. Tentatively, I touch my tongue to the purple head, and you push me roughly to the floor, where I sprawl on my sore ass.

"I thought so, you *sssslut*." You draw out the final barb, sliding on the *s*, the point of the *t* hitting me across the face with your spittle. "Get up," you say. I struggle to stand. My legs weak from yearning pushed to its limits, I'm dazed and determined when I grab at myself, pull the hood of skin back, and start pinching my clit. You smack my hand away, but I don't care, automatically bringing my hands back to position. My lips are parted, wet, and I draw a quick breath between my teeth. Your cock sways, watching my every move.

You grab me and pull me down again across your naked lap. You slip into my dripping slit with no resistance. At last. Your strong, cool hand comes down again and again—your thrusting hips in perfect syncopation. You smack and smooth my pink ass, murmuring sweet obscenities, that I'm getting what I deserve, bucking into me, my juice smeared across your lap. I *am* bad, and this is so good. My eyes roll back into my head, and the heat from where our bodies connect burns there, red behind my eyelids. Pulsing with my blood.

I am a little girl caught masturbating in church, tiny fingers twisting beneath her Sunday dress. I am splayed across my father's pinstriped lap, alive with senses—the musk of his sweat and aftershave, the feel of his worn-leather palm smacking my naked ass. I am screwing my boyfriend in the family room, watching my mother's pacing silhouette on the stairs, calling down to me to please, *please* be a good girl. I am kneeling on cold, hard tile while they strip me, shame me, until I'm back in my pink bedroom, sobbing and squirming against my hand.

I am coming.

• • •

I sat on the edge of the bed, purged of this fantasy, out of breath. You stood across the room, and the outline of your cock pressed endlessly against your worn corduroys. You walked slowly toward me, grabbed my hair in your hand, pulling my head back to look up at you. Firm. Delicious.

"So, is this what you want?" you asked.

"Please," I said.

Grenadine

HANNE BLANK

When her fingers split the fruit, he almost gasped. She looked up for a moment and smiled, then down again into the dish that lay before her on the table, ruby crystal drops spilling from the cleft pomegranate, raining with a soft purr into the shallow glass bowl. The parchment-colored inner membrane clung to irregular pockets of seeds as she broke off a piece and held it up for him to see. Pale pith connected each seed to the fruit, the walls of each garnet-colored drop shaped by its neighbors, packed in tight.

"Like a honeycomb," he said.

She shook her head. "Not at all. Like a woman."

She closed her eyes when she bit, indelicately, whole-heartedly, greedily using her lower lip to coax the seeds into her mouth. He almost blushed to hear the bursting, subtle crunches between her teeth. Several of her fingertips wore red-purple, ringing her cuticles, the space beneath the filed half-moons of the tips. She swallowed, then opened her eyes, a sear of juice sheer and wet and lusciously blood-dark on her lower lip, and she smiled.

"So you've never had one?"

"Not yet," he replied.

Precise as a surgeon, she peeled away membrane, paper-thin, shallow dimples making a net to show where each acid-sweet jewel had been hidden. Bending back the peel, her fingers spread the fruit, seeds fanning to either side of the ridge, the quiet noise of the fruit's flesh yielding like a spade biting sand. She took her time, mouth open against the piece of the pomegranate like a lover, lingering; inhaling the clean, barely bitter breath of its skin as her tongue flicked droplet after taut droplet from its moorings. Strange envy flirted with his belly as her eyebrows lifted, her nostrils flared, her chin lifted just far enough for him to watch the private motions of her throat as she chewed, as she swallowed. He had hoped, when he arrived, that he might be the object of her dedicated hunger.

"You're in for a treat, then."

He cleared his throat quietly, shifting his weight. "It looks that way."

As if she did not know what kept his hands below the table, she leaned toward it, reaching forward, cracking the remains of the section of pomegranate in two with her fingers, holding the redness up toward his lips, toward the sunlight that came in from the window above his head. Ruby prisms caught the light, her fingertips blushing with reflected glory. He licked his lips and leaned forward and then forward still more until the thick wooden tabletop pressed hard just under his ribs so that he had to work to breathe. Licking the residue of drying juice from her lip, she watched him.

He had asked her what she wanted him to bring her from California. "Pomegranates," she had replied without hesitating. His voice had arched like his eyebrow, inquisitive. She had repeated herself slowly, her tone rich, smooth vowels slipping into his ear like lovers slipping into a darkened doorway, their tenancy voluptuously, fabulously transient. "Pom... e... gran... ates."

But the gift had seemed too humble to him, the hard, mottled leather of the dense spheres too graceless. He had had the greengrocer choose them, and hoped that they were good. He wouldn't know. The serrated flaps of pithy tissue at each blossom end seemed to mock his ignorance, looking like some sort of bottle cap, a fantastical finial on a cork he wouldn't begin to know how to remove. With the fruit in a plastic bag, he went into a shop whose high white walls were backdrop to spare, elegant glass shelves lit from below, each pristine glass slab holding a single purse or a couple of scarves or a small, extravagant tangle of python-banded wristwatches arranged artistically, self-consciously, as obviously intended for scrutiny as if they had been on microscope slides. He thought of her hair, dark as her voice, and of the translucence of the skin above her breasts where the veins showed through like looking at a river through the ice, and chose a scarf the blue of the sky just before the first star.

She had untied it with delight, the heavy, hard orbs inside the silk making her beam with anticipation. "Oh, they're gorgeous!" she gushed, and he felt slightly cheated: The scarf had been terrifically dear by comparison to the soft-ball-sized fruit he had wrapped in it. Vanishing into the kitchen, she returned with a bowl, placing two of the pome-granates at the far end of the table and the third into the shallow glass dish.

"Shall we share one now?" she asked, rather rhetorically he thought, pulling out a chair for him. He sat, gamely smil-ing, not sure how to console himself for the fact that she seemed to be more excited to see the pomegranates than to see him. From behind him she leaned down, kissed his cheek, her hands on his shoulders in a firm, affectionate squeeze, and warm, strong fingers sliding down his arms. He sighed, smil-ing tiredly, permitting himself—even as he thought it vain—to believe for a moment that this was a sign that she really was glad, gladder than perhaps she wanted to show, that he was back. It was so hard to tell with something so new, and hard to tell with someone like her, but perhaps it was true.

He closed his eyes at the feel of her breath on his neck, her cheek against his ear, settling back toward her body, her fine warm body, round and sleek. "Sssh," she said when he startled to feel the fluid, cool density of silk on his wrist. She pulled his wrists back gently, as if guiding him to touch her, silk wrapping around the other forearm with sensuous sim-plicity. "Just let me."

He did, the pang of separation almost audible when she walked away and left him on his side of the table, a plucked cello string that shimmered echoing in the resonant chambers of his soul. And he waited, watching, while she began to eat the fruit, until she offered it to him. She didn't move it away as he struggled to get closer, her sweater-sheathed elbows not budging from their spots on the tabletop as he arched his torso awkwardly toward her without pausing to think. Just that, to taste the gems in her fingers, seemed suddenly the point of it all, the hidden goal of the long hours of travel, the long days of waiting until she called him at his hotel, finally, and whispered viscous, buckwheat-honey words into his ear that made him gasp uncontrollably and squirt nine days of work-filled frustration into the Sheraton's starchy sheets.

She did that to him—made him react without thinking, bypassing his cautions, his roadblocks and checkpoints, a master thief who delighted in her own artistry, spilling out the bag of rubies in front of him with such easy grace that he could only wonder how he had ever presumed to own them. Pushing himself harder against the rim of the table, he strained his neck toward her hands, feeling his body pleading suddenly, his eyes widening, imploring, mouth open but still too far away to taste what she held. He felt his ears burning as he fell back into his seat, her implacable soft smile mocking him gently. Her dark eyes, impenetrable, fell on his as she plucked one red kernel from the fruit and placed it between her lips, holding it delicately between her small white teeth, teasing it with her tongue as he watched her. As if her tongue-tip were on his flesh rather than the seed, perhaps on his lower lip, at the notch of his collarbone, he breathed in with his nostrils flaring as she bit down and crushed it.

"Try again," she said, still proffering the fruit. Eyes stinging with cross-country fatigue, he blinked at her, at himself for his silent and instant agreement, leaning toward her out-stretched hand again. Smooth shoe soles slipping slightly on the muted tans and greens of the carpet, he tried to raise himself up, to get a better angle, to win the extra inch or two that would close the gap, his hands useless but straining, fingers gripping hard to opposite forearms, behind his back. Her smile flickered brighter, though her gaze remained impassive, unreadable. She could, he realized, see everything: The French doors at his back were a fine mirror.

With a grunt he lurched forward, managing to press his lips against the fruit, startled to feel how smooth and resilient the round seed-tips were against his lips. Somehow he had expected, even wanted, them to be more delicate, more fragile, to burst against his mouth, drenching him in their juice. A soft groan left his throat unbidden, followed by another desperate lunge, his teeth sinking into small, shocking explosions of tart juice.

Heart pounding, blood rushing, he smiled triumphantly as he chewed, looking into her eyes as he sat back with a heavy thud into the chair. A bead of juice trailed from his lip along his chin, dropping fat and vivid onto his white shirtfront before he noticed a purplish-red inkblot spreading out near the pocket of his button-down. She rose from her chair, staring at it, at him, her expression an odd mixture of challenge and hunger that made him realize quite suddenly that somewhere along the way he had become rock-hard.

Slipping between him and the table, leaning into him and pushing him back against the chair, she straddled his thighs, her skirt taut. He thought that she might kiss him, but instead her tongue found the juice on his chin, scouring it off, her cool, stained fingers slipping between the buttons of his shirt, releasing buttons from buttonholes as they moved down his body to his waist. He moaned at the sensation of her inquisitive tongue, probing the corner of his mouth for hidden juice, at the feeling of her breasts, her belly pressed against his skin as she bared it. And then the sharp splatter, the instant of resistance followed by a bursting liquid half second, the pressure of her thumb on his chest once, then twice, three times—pomegranate seeds she'd hidden in the palm of her other hand crushed one by one against his body.

"You're getting juice everywhere," he said softly, alarmed, slightly shocked, yet helpless.

"No, *you* are," she replied and, looking down, he realized it was true. As if he'd been shot, trickles of red streaked his chest, his belly, their stain dripping down from concentrated bursts where the pulp and the white kernels clung. Juice soaked into his shirt, trailed tickling to his waistband where the dark hairs on his belly became mired in the stuff, slicked with the sweet tartness. She smiled at him, a naughty-girl smile, a knowing smile, the smile of a woman who knows it and does it and gets away with it anyway. "So it's a good thing that you don't mind."

• • •

She slid off of his lap with a soft shimmy of her hips, smoothing her rumpled skirt back down with her hands. But for the soft, self-satisfied grin that curved her lush, red-stained lips, she might've been alone as she sat back down in her chair, her thumbs hooking into the flesh of the broken-open fruit to liberate more of its succulence. She ate with relish, with the unselfconscious grace of great enthusiasm, pausing periodically to suck juice from her fingers or rescue a fallen seed from the dish or tabletop, taking no notice of her bound, spattered paramour across the table or the way he watched her as she devoured the fruit.

He was speechless—or perhaps not, he thought, as he sat in dumb silence. Perhaps it was just that there was nothing to say. He was, after all, quite weary after the long plane ride, the annoyance of the taxi to her apartment, the strange, unbalancing hot-and-cool of her reception, and there was little point in arguing. She would decide what happened next, clearly. As she always did. The thought reassured him, the knowledge that she only appeared to ignore him, that, in reality, she was probably monitoring his every move, gauging his reactions, noting the way he winced slightly as the juice dried, sticky and taut, on his skin. He could fight it or give in to it, give in to the knowledge that she thought of him as hers, as her toy to play with, her very own possession, a cross between pet and lover. He was too tired to fight it.

Perhaps she could see it in the way he sat, in the lassitude that let his spine slump and his arms hang limper than they had before. "I imagine you thought I was going to lick that juice off of you," she said plainly, as if speaking to no one in particular. His cock twitched at the sound of her voice, his eyelids flying open to see her studiously peeling membrane from one of the few remaining pockets of seeds. "I suppose you might well be sitting there imagining the hot, soft velvet of a tongue on your chest even now. Probably you are, thinking about feeling my breath on your skin, my lips suckling juice off you. I know it tickles when it dries."

She nibbled a row of pomegranate seeds from their pocket, mindfully chewing the nibs for a moment as he shifted his weight, feeling his cock straining against his briefs as he thought—as she knew he would—of her tongue, her lips, her hands on his skin. He could feel the light vapor of her breath on his belly, sense memory of the cool evaporation making tiny goose bumps ripple across his chest, shiver on his arms. Before he had gone away she had fucked him hard, pinning him ruthlessly and riding his cock to the point of delirium and past it, biting his chest in the midst of some unnumbered cry, half anguish, half delight. He looked down at the spot where the bruise had remained, trying to decide whether he could still see a faint mark or whether it was only pomegranate juice, shivering slightly deep in the core of his body at the recollection of the pleasure and pain, the remembrance of her lust and the way she used him to feed it. Drifting, he let his eyes close, the better to remember the sensations, the better to imagine them.

"Don't think I don't know you well enough to know what you want," she continued after a pause, her voice lower, slightly mocking as it rumbled with the slightest edge of a sharp-clawed purr. He shivered, unexpectedly, embarrassingly, feeling the little tugging of hairs trapped in dried juice as the skin of his belly twitched, flinched with desire and tension. And then there was pressure on his thigh, a hand, her hand. Firm, showing him where she wanted him, shifting in his seat without opening his eyes. He *wanted* to open them, to look at her bending over him, to see the soft inner curve of her breast,

the heartbreakingly sharp Cupid's bow of her upper lip, to see
if he could divine her next move from the look in her deep-
brown eyes. But his eyelids seemed heavy, reluctant to open,
unwilling to know where or whether he would be touched.

Her tongue was wide and wet and warm as she licked
one slow stripe up his stomach, over his solar plexus. A moan
dried into a whimper as her saliva dried on his skin, his eagerness for another touch, any other touch, transparent. He
could hear his wristwatch ticking, his skin rippling with
subtle sensation, phantom brushes with imaginary hands.
Then teeth, real and hard, scraped down over his nipple,
down the side of his belly, tongue scouring the flesh in rough
circles as he yelped, then thanked her, and unthinkingly
began to beg. He begged her not to stop, to please keep touching him, not to make him wait any longer—to please let him
feel her, to let him please her, to let him do something for her,
anything that would make her happy. As she feasted on his
skin, her hands roaming beneath his shirt, her nails leaving
comet-tails of icy, glittering sensation behind them, he
gasped, called her name, shook as if he were having a seizure,
back arched, head back, almost in orgasm, torn open by her
appetite and his need for it.

And then she was straddling his lap again, his face in her
cleavage as she reached down behind him and tugged at the
silk. The knot came free, his hands falling toward his sides,
helpless and not wanting it otherwise as she stroked his hair,
kissed him, licked the stubble on his jaw to relish the salt, the
grit of him. Held against her body, he sighed a slow, long sigh,
happy just to breathe her in, happy to feel her taking his

measure, reacquainting herself, making pleased little noises as she found the spot just in front of his ear that she liked to kiss.

"You'll be here for a while now—yes?"

He mumbled, nodding, incoherent.

"Good," she affirmed, tilting his head up to look at his face. His eyes opened slowly, bleary, bloodshot, searching. Her red-tinged fingernail traced a dark-pink line down his chest from collarbone to nipple, the juice licked clean but the stain still there. He followed her fingertip as it traced other paths, one then the other, down to the waist, looking up from her hand to her eyes as she slid her finger into his waistband. She beamed, slightly, strangely shy, through juice-stained lips, the dark pink of her smile matching the dark pink streaks on his skin, the single tattletale splash on the shirtfront over his heart, the ruddy finger that hooked beneath his belt and pulled him to his feet and tugged him toward her bed, both of them stained by the same fine juice, so indelible, so shocking, so sweet.

Spa Day

KRISTINA WRIGHT

The little bell over the door tinkled as Marie entered the salon. The cool, refreshing scent of eucalyptus and mint assailed her senses, and she inhaled deeply. The cream-and-white interior was dim, recessed lighting placed strategically to highlight the reception area and the long hallway to the treatment rooms beyond. The reception desk was vacant, the shiny silver counter gleaming and uncluttered.

A door closed somewhere at the back of the salon, and an attractive man in a white T-shirt and gray slacks appeared in the hall. He walked toward Marie, his chest impossibly broad beneath his shirt, his trim waist and thighs hugged by his pants. Marie felt her heart flutter in her chest when he smiled.

"Good morning, Mrs. Vittorio. Are you ready for your massage?"

She nodded. "I'm ready, Mr.—?"

"Call me Robert, " he said easily. "Follow me and I'll get you set up."

Marie followed him down the quiet hall, letting her gaze drift to his ass. The gray slacks only accentuated the muscular curve of his backside. She felt her nipples harden and a tingle begin between her legs. She was going to enjoy this massage very much.

Robert led her into an even darker room where a massage table dominated the floor space. A single light overhead highlighted the table. A white robe and two towels were laid across a nearby chair. Marie could already feel the stress leaving her body.

"You may disrobe now. Wrap a towel around your body and climb up on the table," Robert said. "I'll be back momentarily."

Marie nodded.

Robert started toward the door, then paused. "By the way, I believe there are some open appointments this evening if you'd like to try another of our services."

"Such as?"

"Oh, perhaps a manicure and pedicure. Maybe one of our special facial treatments or an herbal wrap," Robert suggested.

Marie raised an eyebrow. "I'll think about it."

With a nod, Robert left the room.

Marie quickly stripped out of her clothes, eager to relieve herself of the tension and tightness of a long work week. The room wasn't chilly, but she shivered anyway as she removed her bra, imagining Robert's eyes on her. The idea of paying a sexy man to touch her naked body was somewhat arousing.

She had just climbed on the table, her hair pulled up in a loose bun and her towel demurely in place, when Robert returned. A hand towel was slung over his shoulder and he carried a bottle of massage oil. "Are you ready to begin?" he asked, the deep timbre of his voice reverberating through the room.

Marie nodded and closed her eyes.

Silently, he took his place by the table. She heard him open the bottle and the scent of vanilla filled the air. A moment later his warm, wet hands were gliding across her shoulders. His fingers lightly kneaded her muscles, working them with a precision found only in musicians and craftsfolk. She could feel the tightness ease from her body as his fingers coaxed the knots in her neck and shoulders to unwind. She moaned softly in her throat. Embarrassed by her animalistic response, she tucked her head against her arm.

"Relax," Robert soothed. "Let go."

He pushed her towel lower, his fingers quickly covering her skin. Across her shoulder blades, into the stiff muscles at the middle of her back, Robert worked his special brand of magic. Lower, lower, into those spots that ached when she had PMS or had been standing too long. He worked her oil-slick flesh with the hands of a master, his strong fingers driving tension from her body and leaving only a sweet pain.

She was whimpering by the time the towel fell away and he began kneading her buttocks. She clenched the cheeks of her ass as his hands worked them, heat suffusing her face as she felt wetness gather between her legs. He applied more oil to her ass and upper thighs, working it in, making her squirm.

"Does that feel good?" he asked, his fingers straying up her thigh, massaging the crease of her ass, so close to her pussy.

She nodded against her arm, unable to speak.

"Good. Relax."

She didn't feel relaxed. She could feel a new kind of tension building in her body. She wanted to move against his hands. She wanted to raise her ass and spread her legs, begging him to touch her there, where she was hot and wet. Instead, she forced herself to remain still, feeling every push and tug of his hands on her damp skin.

He continued silently, working down the backs of her legs, massaging her thighs and calves until she whimpered softly against her arm. He spent a long time on her feet, manipulating different pressure points until her feet felt as boneless as the rest of her. She thought she felt him press his lips to her instep, but she knew it was probably only her fevered imagination.

"Turn over, Mrs. Vittorio," he said, his voice containing an authoritative note she hadn't heard before. It made her forget her modesty. It made her want to beg for something more than a massage.

She turned onto her back, the towel slipping from beneath her to fall to the floor. She didn't care. She liked being naked beneath Robert's steely gaze, the light above the table shining on her like a spotlight. She stretched her arms above her head and spread her legs just a bit, enough to make her pussy clench as the air hit it.

She watched Robert for a moment, saw the warm appraisal in his steady gaze. Then she closed her eyes and gave herself up to him, trusting him to make her feel good. He began with the tops of her feet, a gentle touch swirling up and around her ankle bones. His hands moved over her shins and kneecaps, then higher to massage the front of her thighs. Her pussy was so wet that she was dripping on the table, but she was beyond caring. All that mattered was this moment and the hands on her body. *His* hands.

His gentle touch slid up past her pubic mound, and she wanted to cry out and ask him to touch her there, but she didn't. He continued the massage with her tummy, his warm hands covering her skin with a soothing touch. Self-consciously, she tightened her stomach muscles, only to have him lay his hand palm-down against her navel.

"Relax. You're beautiful," he murmured, dipping his finger into her navel and swirling oil into the indentation.

She shivered, imagining his fingers dipping into her cunt and finding her own natural moisture. She took a breath and could smell her scent mingling with the vanilla. The room was starting to smell like sex. She wondered if he could smell her.

Slowly, Robert worked his way up her body. He massaged her sides, careful not to linger on her tickle spot. Across her upper abdomen, a gentle, calming touch. Her nipples were already tightly drawn in anticipation by the time his palms covered her breasts. She couldn't hold back a moan of pleasure as he cupped and kneaded her breasts, pushing them together and then drawing them apart. He made circles on her breasts, much like a breast exam only much more sensual. The oil allowed his fingers to glide over her fevered flesh, his touch gentle and firm. He moved up to her collarbone, then to her shoulders, but she could still feel his heat on her breasts, her nipples aching for his touch.

He moved as if to step away and she impulsively reached for his hand. "Here," she said, putting his hand over one breast. "I still feel some soreness."

He made a *tsking* sound low in his throat and began massaging her breast. His fingers sent waves of pleasure throughout her body and she moaned. Soon, his hands covered both breasts, and she squirmed in the mixture of sweat, oil, and pussy juice beneath her. She whimpered when his fingers plucked at her nipples. She moaned when he tugged harder, forcing them up and away from her breast. When he released them, they stood tall and stiff, aching for his touch once more.

"Spread your legs," he said so softly that she wasn't sure she heard him correctly.

Slowly, she spread her legs as far as the narrow table would allow. She inhaled sharply when he moved down the table and stared up between her legs. She could feel how wet she was, but could he see? Judging by the heat in his gaze, he could.

He touched her gently, two fingers on her mound, swirling in her curls. She whimpered when he trailed those fingers around her clit and down to her opening. She couldn't help arching a bit as his fingers touched her pussy, wanting to pull him into her, wanting to feel something inside where she ached.

"Do you want me to finish the massage?" His fingers teased her opening.

She nodded. "Yes, please. I need it."

He eased his fingers into her, chuckling softly. "Oh yes, you do seem to be very tense here."

She raised her hips, taking his fingers deeper. This was what she needed, this sense of fullness. She could feel her wetness surrounding him like hot oil, drenching him in her arousal. Soon, two fingers weren't enough. She needed more.

As if sensing her need, he pushed a third finger into her cunt. "Relax," he said. "Relax."

She tried to obey, taking a deep breath and willing the tension to flow out of her body. She focused all her attention on the fingers inside her, massaging the walls of her pussy, sliding over her G-spot and making her tingle. She closed her eyes, and her world shrank to the space between her legs and the sensations he was causing in her.

He finger-fucked her like that for a long time, working his fingers in and out of her wetness. She could hear the squishy wetness every time he withdrew his fingers and plunged them in again. The sound aroused her even more, driving her desire higher than she could ever remember. She needed this so badly. She needed what only he could give her.

"You can take more," he told her. "You can. Relax."

When he eased a fourth finger into her cunt, she thought she would come on his hand. He went slowly, so slowly she couldn't tell where she ended and he began. She was whimpering loudly now, unashamed of her need. She squirmed on the table, urging him to go faster, harder. But he kept to his slow, methodical pace, filling her with his fingers. Slowly, he slid them out and back in again, over and over in the rhythm of a ballad, steady and sweet.

Her cunt stretched to accommodate his fingers, and there was no pain. There was only this driving need for more. More of him inside her. More of his hand. The image of his hand inside her flooded her cunt with even more wetness. She could feel it trickling down her ass, pooling beneath her. She wanted all of him. She wanted his hand.

"More," she whispered. "Please. More."

He hesitated and she opened her eyes. His expression was dark with lust. "Are you sure?"

"Please."

He nodded.

She closed her eyes and felt him trickle oil over her mound and the fingers inside her. She spread her legs wider, letting them slide off the table. She was spread as wide as she could be, open to his touch, his hand.

"Take a breath. Relax. I'll go slow," he said. His fingers continued to glide into her, wetter and slicker because of the oil mixing with her own wetness. "Breathe. Feel me."

She did as he said, breathing slowly, evenly, feeling the heat of his body so close, feeling only his hand touching her. He held still, so still that she couldn't feel his fingers except when she took a breath. She whimpered impatiently, her body as relaxed as it could be, her mind on edge, waiting, wanting.

He shifted slightly and she began to feel the fullness of his hand. She felt stretched, impossibly so, beyond her body's capacity. He stilled again and she breathed, her breath coming in long, deep pants punctuated by soft moans. Her voice, his hand…there was nothing else, no other stimulus. Her eyes were closed, darkness pulling her down so far inside herself that she wasn't sure she'd ever surface.

"Now. Take me now."

He pushed into her. Her body was impaled on his fist. Her thigh muscles tensed, cramped, then the pain passed and there was only fullness. Complete and utter fullness. She had taken his hand.

"Open your eyes and look at yourself," he said softly.

Her eyelids fluttered open slowly, heavily, as if even her eye muscles were too relaxed to work properly. She raised her head slightly, tucking her arm behind her head so that she could see. The overhead light glinted sharply off the golden hairs of his arm. His strong, muscular forearm flexed, and she felt it deep inside her cunt. She moaned.

"Look," he demanded.

She saw the way his arm angled toward her, the wetness of oil and her own juices slick on his wrist, matting the hair on his arm. And then, her body began. Her cunt, red and engorged, around his hand. From this angle she couldn't see the way he entered her, but she could imagine it. She could imagine the way the lips must be stretched obscenely around his fist, cradling him deep inside her body. She felt her cunt contract on his hand, saw the flicker of pain in his eyes, and felt a surge of need so strong that she moaned.

"Fuck me. God, fuck me," she gasped, rocking her body on his hand.

He fucked her slowly, his hand pumping her cunt with a steady, hard motion that sent tremors through her body. She'd been so close for so long, her orgasm overtook her like his fist had—so slowly she wasn't sure where it began. Suddenly, she was there, one hand clenched around his wrist, the other gripping the table so that she wouldn't fall off. She rocked on his fist, hard, fucking herself on the hand impaling her body, screaming his name over and over as he made her come.

She opened her eyes, watched his expression of lust and pain as her cunt gripped him, tightening on him as she came. She smiled, a feral grin of power and desire, wanting to squeeze his fist inside of her until he became a part of her, until she absorbed everything he could give her.

Slowly, even slower than he went into her, his hand slipped from her cunt. She felt empty when his fingers pulled free. Empty and stretched. He helped her pull her legs back up on the table, every muscle in her body relaxed, numb. She lay there, beneath the single light, limp and wet. Satiated.

Her eyes closed. She wanted to sleep. He stood over her for several minutes, caressing her warm, damp body lightly while she recovered from her orgasm. She felt him press a gentle kiss to her forehead, and she opened her eyes.

"Thank you," she whispered, trying to convey everything she was feeling in those two words. It wasn't enough.

"I hope you'll schedule another appointment with me."

She smiled. "Absolutely."

He glanced at his watch. "Your staff will be here in less than half an hour, and I need to get to work."

"Go," she said. "I'll clean up."

"You sure?"

She sat up and groaned at the feeling in her muscles. "It's the least I can do."

"Can I do anything else for you before I go?" he asked as he offered her the robe from the chair.

"Only one thing…" she said. "I might want one of those special facial treatments at home tonight."

He executed a sharp bow. "Yes, Mrs. Vittorio. My pleasure, ma'am."

"You bet it will be, Mr. Vittorio."

Cast of Three
EMILIE PARIS

My husband and I work at home. Jonathan is a webmaster and I'm a freelance writer. Some of our friends tease us, winking as they wonder aloud if we lounge all day in silk pajamas and satin robes. If they only knew....

On a recent Friday morning, while I was speaking on the phone with one of my editors, Jonathan came into my office. His faded khakis were open at the fly, and his unbuttoned denim work shirt revealed his broad chest, muscular from many hours of nightly workouts. I met his gaze and instantly understood the yearning, hungry look in his eyes. As I continued talking to Fiona, I watched Jonathan take out his cock and begin stroking it slowly, deliberately.

My editor, oblivious on the other end of the line, spoke to me of dashes and commas, of new paragraphs and run-on sentences. All the while, Jon's hand worked faster on his cock, the ridge of his palm slamming against his body as skin moved on skin. That clapping sound was undeniably erotic, and I could feel a rush of heat color my cheeks. I love watching my husband jerk off. His brow furrows. His sea-green eyes squeeze shut. Near the end, his head goes back, revealing the seductive line of his long neck. I can see him swallow hard, steel himself as he tries not to let loose. Then, as he approaches his peak, he talks. Murmurs, really. Nonsense words, or unfinished words. Sometimes he says my name, whispers it.

Fiona was saying it now. *"Gina,* are you listening?"

"I'm fine," I said. "I mean, I'm here. Could I—?" I was starting to say, "Could I call you back?" but Jonathan stopped me, shaking his head quickly as he took a step in my direction. He didn't want me to get off the phone.

"Could you repeat that last bit?" I asked, shooting him a questioning glance.

He answered with actions rather than words. Moving closer, he placed the head of his throbbing cock against my glossed lips, butting forward. I sucked him easily, the phone still cradled in my hand, his cockhead cradled between my parted lips. The tip of my pink tongue flicked out, up and down his shaft. While I worked him, I tried not to make any noise, moved away from him when I had to give a response to Fiona.

With my focus shifted from Fiona to fucking, I could no longer comprehend what my editor was saying, but I was still able to make those *mm-hmmm* comfort sounds that tend to appease her. She continued speaking to me about a recent project, one that she'd liked but that needed minor changes. Changes like the shift and pull of Jon's cock in my mouth, minor edits like the way he dragged the head of his cock along the roof of my mouth, reveling in the ridged texture against his smooth skin.

Finally, Fiona said, "That's about it, Gina. Call me when you have a fresh draft."

"Mm-hmmm," I said again, pulling back from Jon and adding a "good-bye" before hanging up the phone. I thought my husband would ravish me then and there. I was sure he'd turn me around in the leather office chair, lower my well-worn jeans, place the slick, wet head of his cock between my slender thighs, and enter my dripping pussy. A good, satisfying fuck is one of my all-time favorite ways to start the day. But Jon had other ideas. Leaning across my desk, he asked, "What's Victoria's number?"

"Why?" I asked. Already, I had one hand between my legs, cupping my cunt through the crotch of my jeans, rocking on the seam that pressed perfectly against my clit. I could already sense how good this climax was going to be.

"Just tell me."

His cock pointed forward, like a divining rod. I blinked, thought of my ex-roommate's number, and rattled it off from memory before realizing what he was doing. Yet, somewhere in my head, I knew. Of course I knew. This was one of Jonathan's four-star fantasies in motion. And all I had to do was play along.

While I watched, he dialed the number quickly and then handed me the phone. "Victoria Morris, please," I said when the receptionist answered. As I talked my way through Vicky's personal assistant, Jon moved me around, so that my ass was toward him. Swiftly, he lowered my jeans down my thighs, leaving them on but out of his way.

"I liked the way you handled Fiona," he said, as I waited for Vicky to answer the phone. "See if you can keep it up."

Vicky is a high-level attorney, but I knew she wouldn't mind a call at work. Still, I couldn't immediately think of anything to say as Jon's cock worked its powerful way into my tight cunt. He had one hand around my waist, and his fingers lingered lightly between the lips of my pussy. Luckily, when Vicky came on the line, I had a sudden brain wave.

"Hey, Vick," I said. "I was wondering if we could have lunch together Friday."

"Let me check my schedule." I could hear the beeping from her electronic date book. As she scrolled through the week, she said, "How's life at home? You guys getting any work done, or are you just fucking around?"

"I'm getting a lot taken care of," I said, grinning, feeling those wondrous inner muscles of my pussy begin to helplessly contract on the head of Jon's cock. At this move, his breathing grew more ragged. I looked into the window above my desk and could see a ghostly reflection of the two of us. My long, auburn hair was pulled back in a no-nonsense ponytail, and as I watched, Jon pulled the ribbon free, letting my curls fall loose around my shoulders. He gripped into my hair with one hand, pulling my head back hard. Feeling the power behind that move, I wondered how long I'd be able to keep up a normal-sounding conversation.

Vicky had found Friday at last. "I've got a mid-morning meeting that might go late. How's one o-clock?"

"One's great," I managed to answer. "I'll meet you in the lobby."

"Got another call, Gina. Be good," she said, and she was gone.

Be *good?* As good as I could possibly be, as good as anyone could be in that situation. I was rocked with the motions of Jon's body against mine. His cock slammed forward and then withdrew, leaving just the mushroom head inside me. The scent of my arousal was light in the air. Jonathan always says my pussy smells like perfume, like flower petals, but I don't agree. I think I have a richer scent—slightly spicy—just before I come. And right now, I was about to come. Jon sensed it. Grabbing my waist, he pulled me back against him. My office chair has wheels at the bottom, and the whole piece of furniture moved with me, rocking us both. Jon seemed to like that, and he gripped the arms of the chair and fucked me using the motion of the wheels. Then, his breathing harsh, he said, "Call Sarah."

"Come on, Jon." I was dying, caught in the moment of not wanting to come because it felt so good but almost coming anyway because I couldn't fucking help it. If he would just keep up the rhythm, I'd climax in no time.

"Call her, Gina."

"Please," I said. "I'm almost there."

"Just call her up."

Jon knew I was stalling for time, just playing with him. He brought his hand down on my rear, giving me a playful love-spank to make me obey. I hesitated for one more moment, winning myself another spank before caving in to his desires.

My ass smarted from the open-handed smack, and I reached back to rub the sore spot before lifting the phone.

Sarah's our next-door neighbor. I have her number on our speed dial and, staring into Jon's reflection, I picked up the handset and pressed one button. She's an artist and works at home, too. I could hear her phone ringing through the connecting wall of our townhouses.

"Talk dirty this time," Jon said, grabbing my asscheeks with both hands, pawing me hard enough to leave marks.

"Dirty?"

"You know, baby."

He was right. I knew. As I said, this was Jon's favorite fantasy in motion, an X-rated sex play with a cast of three. Who was I to knock it off course? I held the phone to my ear and waited, impatiently, for Sarah to answer. She picked up on the fifth ring.

"Hey, it's Gina," I managed to squeak out as Jon pulled his cock, wet and sticky, from my cunt and began making thrusting moves with the head between the cheeks of my ass. I trembled, knowing exactly what he was going to do and wondering how I was going to talk through it.

"What's up, girl?"

My heart rate, I thought. "Nothing," I said, "just procrastinating."

"Still in your pajamas?"

Jon moved back and forth, rubbing the length of his rock-hard cock along the split of my ass before oiling it up with his spit and thrusting the first inch inside me. I would have moaned aloud if I hadn't been talking to Sarah. Instead, I said, "PJs? You think I wear pajamas?"

"You're right, Gina," she said apologetically. "You're much more of a T-shirt and panties kind of girl."

"How about you?" I asked, envisioning her thick black hair falling over her shoulders, her slender body draped in something long and sheer and silky. "What are *you* wearing?"

"Nothing," Sarah said, and her voice sounded as raw as Jon's. I could tell that my kinky husband liked the way this conversation was going, because he suddenly slipped in another inch of his bone. I bit my lip to stifle the sound of a moan as he whispered, "Invite her over."

"How can you paint when you're not wearing any-thing?" I asked, my voice trembling. Jon had stopped moving, his cock now tucked deep in my ass, his hands resting lightly on my waist. I squeezed him rhythmically with my muscles, but still managed to reach forward and press the speaker button on our phone.

"I'm not painting, silly," Sarah said to the captive audi-ence of two. "I'm listening to you guys do it."

"How'd you know...?" I asked, as Jon started moving again inside me.

"The squeak of your wheels against the wood floor. It's got a very familiar sound to it. And he's making you call people again, isn't he?"

"Get over here, kid," Jon said, continuing his throbbing pace in my ass, grabbing the arms of the chair again and letting Sarah hear the squeak of the wheels.

"On my way."

Jon leaned over me to hang up the phone, pressing his cock all the way to the hilt as he did. I sighed and then moaned aloud, no longer playing the role of the hard-working freelancer.

Sarah has a key to our apartment. For emergencies. Or times when we're out of town and she brings in the mail. Or mornings when the three of us decide that what we really need to get done is not our work but each other. The door opened only moments later, and we heard her padding in bare feet down the hall. Quickly, I turned to see my best friend standing in the doorway.

"Now isn't this a pretty picture," she said, smiling. "I should have brought my easel."

Jon motioned for her to join us.

"Where do you want me, Jonny?" Sarah asked. "On the table so I can kiss your pretty wife, or on my knees behind you so I can lick your asshole until you shoot?"

Sarah can talk like a trucker. It's one of her best features, and it was obvious from his expression that Jon didn't know what he wanted. Both scenarios were equally arousing. But after brief consideration, he took a breath and said, "Start with Gina. She needs you."

Did I ever. I needed her perched on my polished wood desk so that I could run my hands up and down her supple body. Needed her pouting lips parted against my own so that I could meet her tongue with mine. She had slipped on a robe, and I nearly tore it in my haste to see her naked. As soon as I did, I realized that she hadn't lied to me. She'd been listening to us fuck, and the sounds had turned her on. I could tell from the way her shaved pussy lips were already glistening with her personal lubrication.

"I want to taste you," I said.

Sarah didn't seem to have a problem with this idea. But she did have a problem with the location. There was no comfortable place for her to sit. Jon took care of the situation swiftly, picking me up while still inside of me and moving me onto the floor. Sarah took up her position in front of me immediately, parting her toned thighs and then staring to see if I would follow through with my offer. I could hardly wait. With Jon slipping back and forth in my ass, I bent and brought my tongue to Sarah's carefully shaved cunt, French-kissing her throbbing clit and making her moan loudly. Luckily, we're the only freelancers in our line of townhouses. There was nobody else to be disturbed by the sounds of us getting together.

"Lick her clit," Jon told me, in the directing mode. "Make her come hard."

That was my plan, exactly. Taking over from where her fingers had obviously left off, I got her up to our speed in no time. My tongue made tricks and spirals and figure-eights around her hot little button. I slid it into her hole and pressed in deep, tongue-fucking her until she was moaning. Then I brought my hands into the action, parting the petal lips of her pussy as wide as they'd go, then slurping and sucking at her with my mouth. Jon couldn't get any harder than he already was, but the scene he was watching had to have some effect on him. So, finally, with a guttural moan, he came, shooting deep into my ass and then staying there, his hands holding me tight, fingers slipping beneath my waist to play a magical melody on my clit.

His knowing rhythm brought me up to the ridge of climax, and as Sarah sealed her pussy to my mouth, I found myself coming. Coming between my husband and my friend in the sweetest, stickiest climax of all time. My body was shaking as I worked to keep licking Sarah. I didn't want her to be left out, now that both Jon and I had reached our limits. In no time, Sarah was gripping my shoulders and bucking against my face. She came long and hard, just as Jon had hoped she would, and the way she tasted was so sweet it was almost unreal.

When we were finished, I was dripping from both ends, my mouth slicked up with Sarah's honeyed nectar, my cunt throbbing, Jon's cream dripping out of me. We lay there all together, entwined on the floor of our office, trying to regain our sense of balance, our memory of how to breathe without panting and speak without moaning.

As I stared up at the ceiling, I thought about what Jon must have done. While I was working like a good girl in my office, he'd undoubtedly called Sarah, reminding her that as it was the third Friday of the month, it was his turn to change fantasy into reality. Sarah had taken up her position in the room closest to my office, listening as she waited for the phone call that would beckon her to our house. Listening and stroking herself as the anticipation built inside her.

This meant that next time, Sarah was up. As if reading my mind, Jon leaned forward on one arm and looked over at our sultry neighbor. "Sarah, it's your turn next week. Do you want to play out the rescue fantasy again, or the one where I burst in on you two dirty, naughty coeds?"

"Let's play free-loving freelancers," Sarah said with a smile. "We'll do all the sexy things people think we're doing when we tell them we work at home."

"If they only knew..." Jon and I said together.

But with Onions

R. GAY

Andrew enjoys chopping onions, and I enjoy watching. He has a ritual—fetching a well-rounded yellow onion from the vegetable drawer, slowly removing the dry husk of peel, holding the onion under cool water to lessen the sting before placing it on a wooden cutting board. There are his hands, thick, veined, pale, and strong, the knife in his hand as if it were simply another finger. He holds the onion between the thumb and forefinger of his left hand and carefully makes almost translucent slices of the onion. He is methodical, gently piercing the onion's flesh with the tip of the knife before bringing down the entire blade, working it through the onion, hitting the cutting board with a satisfying *thunk,* then sliding the fresh slice aside. Occasionally he eats a slice of onion, because Andrew also likes the taste.

When Andrew chops onions, he cries. I sit on the counter, absorbing his lean face, the faint scar that runs from his right eyebrow to just above his upper lip, his crooked nose. I see a thin stream of tears falling from his eyes, down his face, quivering on his chin before falling to his shirt or running down his throat, and I feel a stirring between my thighs, faint at first, growing as he cries harder, and harder. And I feel perverse, because when Andrew chops onions and when Andrew cries he looks beautiful and fuckable and vulnerable, and I am torn between wanting to see more and wanting him to close the short distance between us.

Andrew knows I enjoy watching him chop onions, so the ritual has become a point of seduction between us. As he slices, he will turn slightly toward me, from the corner of his eye watching me press my thighs together. He will flex the muscles of his forearm. He will talk to me, lowering his voice, speaking slowly, making me shiver as the baritone of his words tickles my ears. When he is done, he washes his hands under warm water, dries them with a dishtowel, and arches an eyebrow. I sit perfectly still, unclench my thighs, smile, and inch forward, beckoning him toward me. Andrew will make me wait, leaning against the counter, one foot crossed over the other, his arms loose at his side. He likes doing that, making me wait. He'll stare until I'm uncomfortable, until I've memorized his gaze, until I'm forced to look away. And then he'll slowly walk toward me, and the kitchen feels strangely silent, save for the sound of his bare feet against the tiles, a slightly moist sound that turns the stirring between my thighs into a cruel, slow burn.

He will hold my face between his hands. Again I will notice how thick, veined, pale they are against my much darker skin. He will press his thumbs against my lips, then move them upward, along the lines of my nose, softly across my eyelids, then back to my lips. All the while, I can smell the sting of onion on his skin. And then he is no longer gentle or silent. He will kiss me, hard, until my lips feel bruised and swollen. He will rub his face against mine, and I will taste his tears and the onion on his breath. I will moan, hoarsely, though he hasn't really touched me, not yet—not the way I need him to. I will wrap my legs around his waist, pulling him closer, gnawing on his neck, kissing the hollow of his throat, tasting more tears. My hands will slide under his shirt, and I will desperately grab his chest, enjoying the way his skin feels beneath the palms of my hands. It's a peculiar sensation, for he is not soft but sinewy, and with my eyes closed I imagine I can feel his blood rushing, his lungs gasping, his heart beating. I will pinch his nipples between my fingers, and I will exhale loudly, because I am fascinated by his nipples, small, erect pink disks that interrupt the pale expanse of his chest.

He will open my bathrobe and, forcing his hands between my thighs—for they are again clenched together—he will spread my legs apart, he will spread them until they ache. But I enjoy the ache. It makes me wet. He will bite my shoulders, inhale my breasts into his mouth, pausing to trace my hardened, purple nipples with his tongue as if trying to trace every crease along them. My hands will slide down his torso to the waist of his jeans, and I will fumble with the button, crying in frustration if it catches, then quickly undo the zipper. He will stop, quickly step out of them, move back between my thighs, and I will sigh with relief because for the one moment when he steps away, I feel empty and hungry. Andrew will pull me to the edge of the counter, the sharpness of it digging into my ass, which I will ignore. I will feel the tip of his cock against my navel, and I will wrap my hand around the shaft, feeling the warmth, the pulsing of the thick tendon along the underside, the way it continues to swell.

There will be no more seduction. In one elegant movement, he will position his cock at the entrance of my cunt, and he will thrust forward, burying his head between my breasts. I will want to scream, but instead choke, my voice trapped in my throat. I will tighten my legs around his waist. I will rest my chin against the top of his head. I will clench the muscles of his back with my hands—they are slick, strained—leaving the deep, crescent imprints of my fingernails. Our moans, harsh and low, will echo against the tiles and counters. I will tighten myself around his cock and he will press deeper. I will wish that we could enter each other's bodies. And when we come, we will both cry, and later, lying in the bathtub, scrubbing each other clean, we will say it was the sting of onions in the air.

There are other times—times when, not even halfway through the onion, Andrew will push the cutting board away from him, grab me off the counter, turn me around, and swiftly remove my robe. I will feel the rough denim of his jeans brushing against my ass, shivering as he slowly unbuckles his belt, letting the leather strap slide across my skin. He won't even bother stepping out of his jeans. Instead, he lets them wade around his ankles. There will be no time to waste. He will clasp the back of my neck with his right hand, holding my forehead to the counter, as he moves his left hand along my spine to my ass cheeks, squeezing them hard. He will take the open bottle of olive oil from the counter, slathering a thick layer around his cock, on the puckered opening of my ass. Carefully, but with determination, he will press himself into the tightest part of me, an inch at a time, until he can go no further. I will stop breathing, and become intimately aware of the sound of the sink's leaky faucet. It will hurt, but I like the hurt, welcome it.

I will wonder what I look like from this position; does he find it attractive? I will think that bent over like this, ass exposed, legs trembling, I have become the kind of girl—no, woman—our mothers warned us about in hushed and awkward tones. When he pulls back, leaving just the tip of his cock in my ass, I will gasp for air, having forgotten that I was holding my breath. Now, he will wait, watching me squirm and pant and push myself backward, wanting him back inside me. And then he will slide forward again, grinding his hips in short, punctuated thrusts. The pain will start flowering into pleasure, and I will feel myself loosening around him.

I will hear my voice, but it will sound strange to my ears. I will beg him to fuck me harder, deeper. I will beg him to call me his slut, his whore, his fuck toy; and when he does, my body will shudder, it will nearly throb. My back will arch and I will try to raise my head from the counter, but he will slam it back down. I will feel my clit wet, swollen, and pulsing, and I will beg him to please touch it. *Touch what?* he will ask. *Touch me there,* I will plead. Softly, too softly, he will slide his hand around my waist and down, pausing as he runs his fingers through my pubic hair, then moving lower. He will press two fingers against my clit and hold them there. I will buck my hips, trying to trap his hand between my body and the cabinets below. But he is stronger. And this is all for him. He will lightly feather my clit with the pads of those two fingertips, and I will feel an indescribable sensation, keen, almost unbearable, and it will crawl from my clit through every inch of my skin.

I will feel used. His thrusts become harder, and in addition to the water dripping in the sink, I will hear his sweaty skin slapping against mine. When he comes, it will be fast, and violent. He will forget that I am a person. I am simply a tunnel that he is traveling through. My clit will feel like exploding. When I feel the hot, brief spurts of his cum shooting up my ass, I am the one who will cry. I will not come...but I don't want to, because I like the unsatisfied edge I am left with. I will try to push myself away from the counter, but my damp skin will stick. My arms and legs will feel rubbery, and just before I fall, he will take me in his arms, and I will suckle his fingers into my mouth. I will relish the taste of onions.

Double Vision

MARK BROOKS

"Did I ever tell you," my girlfriend Noelle asked, "about the time I slept with Luke and Tom at the same time?"

We had just finished making love for the second time that night, and the two of us were naked and tangled up in sweat-damp sheets on her bed. I was used to hearing about Noelle's sordid sexual experiences, but I'd never heard about this one. She'd had a much more interesting sex life than I had.

I always loved it when Noelle offered up another tidbit of her deliciously wicked sexual past. It was our favorite game—kiss-and-tell. Noelle giggled when she saw the eagerness on my face. The timeless ritual was begun: Noelle would inflame me mercilessly with tales of her sad, sordid life, then fuck me cross-eyed, bowlegged, and stupid.

"No," I said. "You never did tell me that one," I said.

"Do you want to hear about it?"

"What do you think?" I asked her as her abdomen pressed against my growing hard-on.

Noelle smiled and began. "I was nineteen." That made it almost twelve years ago. "I was a freshman at Berkeley. Luke was the first guy I slept with after I came to college. I guess he was the first guy I knew who was openly bisexual. He had a single room—I had a roommate—so we were always in his room. We used to fuck for hours—I mean, hours and hours and hours. And *hours*. We used to fuck so hard the corners of Luke's bed would put divots in the drywall. People from the next college over would call the campus police to complain. This one time, a crowd of people gathered down in the quad and started applauding when I came.… Are you enjoying this?"

"You're making this up," I said. Noelle's hand had curved around my cock, now fully hard, and as her fingers gently worked their way up and down I moaned.

"You know I don't have to make stuff up," she told me with a smile. "Real life is so much dirtier. I was so embarrassed at the time."

"You? Embarrassed? Impossible."

Noelle squeezed my balls.

"Mercy!" I yelped.

"Then play nice," she said.

"I promise," I said.

"Anyway," sighed the smiling Noelle, stretching out atop me once more with her hand loosely cradling my cock. "Luke had this gay friend named Tom who had been his roommate in the dorms the first year. Tom was *so* cute. I mean, I loved Luke, but Tom was the kind of guy that girls dream about. He was fucking *gorgeous*. OK, so anyway, like I said, I had never known a real bisexual guy—one who'd actually done it, actually fucked around with guys and girls both. The idea of Luke fucking another guy just totally drove me nuts. I used to fantasize about it all the time. I told Luke all about it."

"What did he think?"

"He thought it was hot. Then he told me Tom thought he was bisexual."

"With you around, I can imagine," I said, reaching for her breasts. She caught my hands and pushed them away playfully, though her nipples were obviously hard and she plainly wanted me to touch her. She held my wrists down.

Noelle leaned down, smiling wickedly, and gulped my cock into her mouth. I ran my fingers through her long, dark hair, muttering encouragements.

Noelle's story, coupled with the stimulation of her hand and mouth on my cock and balls, had already brought me to the brink of orgasm.

"You are so hot," I whispered as I lifted myself up, put my hands on Noelle's shoulders, eased her back onto the bed. "Don't stop," I begged as I kissed her mouth, soft at first, then harder, then harder, then harder harder harder until Noelle was arching her back and writhing hungrily underneath me as I bit at her lips and penetrated her with my tongue.

"I'm not sure I can remember the rest of the story," said Noelle absently.

"Remember," I told her firmly. I started kissing my way lower on Noelle's throat, nearing her full, firm breasts. I used my hands to play with the hard nipples.

Noelle told her story only with great difficulty. "One night Luke and I had this evening planned. He had the only TV set and VCR on the hall. I had never seen a porn movie, and he was going to remedy that."

My fingers found Noelle's pussy, and I slipped two fingers into her, biting her nipple roughly as I did. Noelle's spine arched and her ass lifted up off the bed.

"Don't stop or *I'll* stop," I told her as I worked a third finger into her, slid it deeper.

She stifled another moan of ecstasy and continued with her story through rhythmic sounds as I worked her clit with my thumb and thrust my fingers into her. With my other hand, I held my hard cock, excited by the knowledge of what was to come.

"Anyway, when I showed up at Luke's dorm room, Tom was already there. Luke told me Tom had just dropped by, but even then I figured that had to be a setup. Tom said he'd never seen porn either—straight porn, that is—and Luke asked me if it would be all right if Tom stayed to watch it with us."

I lowered my mouth further, letting my warm breath ruffle her pubic hair.

Making it look effortless, Noelle pivoted her body so that her ass was comfortably on the edge of the bed, as far forward as it could go—in the perfect position for me to eat her out. I lowered my mouth to her cunt and pressed my lips to her pussy. I wriggled my tongue into her tight hole, licking hungrily. Noelle moaned as my lips and tongue played around her clit and then traveled back down to her dripping pussy.

"Those dorm rooms were *small*," Noelle continued breathlessly, without prompting, as I licked her. "And so all three of us sat on the bed and watched these porn videos. We started drinking wine, and maybe it helped break the ice. Oh God, right there—that's right, lick my pussy just like that—right there, oh God...."

"Tell me more," I demanded insistently between thrusts of my tongue into Noelle's pussy and twirls of it around her swollen clitoris. I rubbed my naked cock against Noelle's leg, so she could feel how hard I was, how hard she was making me. God, I was harder than I had ever been, and Noelle moaned as she felt my cock against her leg. She tried to bend over, to reach down to take hold of my hard cock, but I slipped my tongue back into her cunt, and she whimpered and relaxed into the bed. "Get this cock of yours in my face," she breathed. "God, I've got to have your cock in my mouth if you want to hear any more of the story," she told me.

"How can you talk with your mouth full?"

"I'll find a way," she said.

The woman knew what she wanted. I climbed onto the bed, assuming a 69 position. I put my mouth on her and started to lick again. Noelle wrapped her hand tightly around my hard cock and stroked it, rubbing the slick head against her face, her lips, her breasts, squirming against me as she talked. I was already incredibly turned on, and Noelle's stroking brought me closer and closer to an orgasm as I licked her closer to hers. I slipped two fingers into Noelle's wet cunt and began to gently finger her as I licked her clit. She moaned.

Noelle wrapped her lips around my cock and started to suck me, and I almost shot into her mouth right there. But I didn't want to come yet—so I fought my orgasm down while she talked.

"Finally, we started making out," she said, her mouth against my cock. "I was so hot for both of them. They both had their hands everywhere. We started taking our clothes off, and nobody said anything, like talking would break the mood. Tom started sucking Luke's cock, and I started sucking his. God, it was hot watching Tom suck Luke off like that." Noelle took a moment to slip my cock into her mouth, and I knew I would come if she didn't stop. So I pressed my mouth to her and started licking her clit, knowing she was going to come herself, my moans telling her how close I was.

I guess she wanted to finish the story: She took her mouth off my cock and started talking fast while she stroked my cock very, very slowly with her hand. I held my orgasm at bay with great difficulty.

"Luke and I started sucking Tom's cock together, trading off on it while Tom jacked Luke off. Tom said he'd never fucked a girl before. Luke asked him if he wanted to, and he said 'Sure.' So Luke got a condom from the nightstand and helped me roll it on Tom."

"I'm going to come," I said.

"Not yet! Not yet! I climbed on top of Tom and put him inside me while Luke and I kissed. I was incredibly turned on. I started fucking Tom while he sucked Luke's dick. I knew I was going to come no matter what I did, so I fucked him really slow and started rubbing my clit. That—that feels so good—right there—keep doing that! I came once and Tom just looked at me like I was crazy, then started laughing. 'I never saw a girl come before,' he said. 'I didn't know you made so much noise!' He wanted to be on top of me, so I rolled onto my back and Tom got back inside me. Then Luke got up alongside the bed and put his cock in my mouth. God, it felt good to be fucking them both. God, I was going to come again—don't stop, don't stop, don't...."

Her ass lifted off the bed, her back arching, her naked body squirming, she came—moaning, gasping, pumping her hips as my mouth rode her clit. She started working my cock with her hand and I came too, my head spinning as the pleasure coursed through me; my come jetted onto her breasts and shoulder. When the two of us ground to a halt, I took a deep breath and started laughing.

"What?" asked Noelle.

"Did it really happen like that?"

Noelle smiled, slipping out from under me. "It was an awfully long time ago," she said. "It might have."

"I see."

"And maybe it happened a different way," she said. "Why don't I tell you the story again tonight...and we can see if anything changes?"

Number One on the List

KATE DOMINIC

Justin and I were at an impasse. We'd decided to spice up our marriage by making lists of things we'd like to try—no holds barred. We could put anything we wanted in one of three columns: interested, OK if you want to, and not interested, with stars by the things we felt really strongly about. Then we were going to make a list, in order, of the five things we'd most like to try.

I wondered what Justin would choose. Although my Internet-whiz husband spent his days in front of a computer screen, he kept in shape by swimming laps at lunchtime at the health club next door to where he worked. Knowing how much he liked being in the pool, I guessed he might want to try skinny dipping. Thinking of his long, lean frame floating naked next to my shorter and extremely busty figure had me all kinds of hot and bothered. I put a star next to skinny dipping on my "interested" list.

But I never dreamed he'd want to try pee play—the *other* kind of watersports. It didn't gross me out or anything. I'd just never considered it to be sexy. I was totally shocked when Justin listed having me pee on him as number one with three stars on his "like to try it" list.

Negotiation has always been the hallmark of our relationship. So when I got over my shock, I took a deep breath and said I'd think about it. I got online and did some research. We talked. I was really embarrassed when Justin said he sometimes surreptitiously sniffed my panties. Now *that* sounded sexy. When I blushed, he picked up the thong I'd just taken off, closed his eyes, and inhaled deeply. The look of bliss on his face turned me on so much I jumped him and we fucked right there on the floor in front of our closet.

But no matter how much the idea of peeing on Justin was starting to intrigue me, I couldn't get turned on by the thought of the mess we'd have to clean up later. Justin had said he'd be glad to take care of things. That still didn't sound like such a hot idea. I like to cuddle afterward. Eventually, though, the more I researched, the more I realized I was going to have to confess the real reason for my hesitation.

I've always been pee shy. Unless my bladder's ready to burst, I can't even go in a public restroom when somebody's in the stall next to me. Even then, when I finally let go, it's just a trickle, just enough to relieve the worst of the pressure. If I was that way around other women, I couldn't begin to imagine peeing around a man, even my husband.

Justin said he understood, but I could tell he was disappointed. The next week, when he left on a business trip, I invited my neighbor, Carol, over for coffee and spilled the beans. She and I both work at home, and we take our breaks together when we need to talk. She's one of those people you can say anything to, and know it won't go any farther. I also knew from her discussions about her own life that she was active in the local fetish scene. As usual, she was sitting at my kitchen table wearing just the bottom of her swimsuit and a see-through cotton tee that reinforced how totally uninhibited she was. Every time she moved, her short brown curls bobbed and her full breasts strained seductively against the well-worn material.

"I bet you think I'm really silly," I blushed, keeping my eyes glued to my cup.

"Sounds pretty normal," she said with a laugh. I looked up to see her grinning wickedly at me. "Lots of people have that problem. It's easy to fix."

"Yeah, right." I set my mug down with a thunk. "Are you telling me I can learn to pee in front of other people?" I shook my head, but this time it was my turn to smile. "No way, Carol. I'm too much of a closet case."

"Are you saying you don't want to try?"

Her question stopped me cold. Carol has a way of nailing you with her steely gaze until you squirm. I suddenly remembered in no uncertain terms why she was such a well-respected dominant in her community. I blushed and rolled the cup in my hands.

"Are you telling me even I can learn to do it?" I countered.

"Sure. I taught a class on it last summer. Um, a private class," she said, winking. "I'd be glad to help you out." Her eyes traveled slowly up and down me, then locked on mine, her interest obvious. I felt as if she'd undressed me with her eyes—and liked what she saw. My face heated again.

"Afterward, I'd be able to...you know," I took a deep breath, "pee for Justin?" My voice came out in a scared little squeak.

"Sure, honey. You want to try?" She eyed me over the top of her glass, and waited.

I looked at her, at the floor, at my mug, and swirled the last of my coffee, all the time thinking of how my pussy had tingled at the look on Justin's face when he sniffed my panties. My face felt as if it was on fire when I finally looked up at her and gulped, "Yes."

Carol's grin made me shiver. She picked up the pot and refilled my cup. "Drink up, Amber. The lesson starts right now."

Five cups of coffee and one multivitamin later, I was squirming in my chair. My jitteriness wasn't only from the caffeine. Carol had assured me that the coffee was just enough of an irritant that I'd really feel inspired to go—especially with that much fluid in my bladder. And the vitamin would make my urine bright yellow. When I had to go so badly I was crossing my legs, she marched me to the bathroom and turned on the shower full blast. She made me stick my hand in to test the temperature.

"Warm enough, Amber?"

"It's fine," I grimaced, bending forward and squeezing my legs together to keep from wetting my pants.

Carol laid her hand gently on my belly, pressing very, very lightly. I groaned, clenching my muscles as hard as I could. She laughed and kissed my forehead lightly.

"I'm going to step outside now, Amber. Close the door and tell me when you're naked." She moved away, but stopped with her hand on the doorknob. "Don't even think of lifting that toilet seat."

"Yes, ma'am," I whispered, almost shutting the door on her in my hurry. I tore off my clothes, then took a deep breath, my legs still squeezed together, and choked out, "I'm ready."

Her voice was muffled, but I could hear her laughing. "I'm going home now, girlfriend. I'll lock the front door behind me. You climb in that shower and stand in that nice warm water until you pee right into it. Don't you dare get out until you go. Let the water flow all over your body, down your breasts and your belly, and between your legs...."

"Good-bye, Carol!" I shouted. Ignoring her hoots of laughter, I hopped in the shower and yanked the glass door closed behind me.

The water hit me with a vengeance. I shuddered so hard every hair on my body stood up. It felt almost good, in a weird sort of way, almost as if I was coming. Damn, I had to go.

It took a long while, though. I forced myself to keep my legs open, just the way Carol had told me to. I couldn't help clenching, even though I had to go so badly. Finally I turned so that the water ran down the whole front of my body. My eyes flew open as a trickle of hot fluid seeped out of me. I looked down between my legs at the bright yellow runnel fading to pale in the water swirling at my feet. I leaned back, letting the water hit between my breasts, so that it fanned out over my belly, warm and relaxing and comfortable. With a whoosh, my muscles let loose and a bright yellow stream gushed out onto the white porcelain floor of the tub. I stayed like that, panting, until my bladder was empty and the shower had rinsed the last evidence away. Suddenly I started to giggle. I climbed out and hurriedly dried off. Wearing only my towel, I rushed to the phone to call Carol. I felt positively wicked. And there wasn't a drop of mess to clean up.

Carol ordered me to stay in my bathrobe all day—in fact, every day until Justin came home—so that every time I had to pee, I could practice. Thank God I didn't have to drink any more coffee, though. Apple juice and water worked just fine. Pretty soon, I was able to hop in and pee without even thinking about it.

The hard part was playing with myself while I did it. Per her directions, I called her with an update each day. On Thursday, she told me to start rubbing my clit just before I went, and to keep rubbing the whole time I peed. I was so embarrassed that my face felt hot, even in the privacy of the shower. But Carol's first set of instructions had worked. And oh God, this one did, too. She'd forbidden me to masturbate, unless I was peeing. Pretty soon, I was so horny that I was drinking extra juice just so that I could hop in the tub more often.

I was really nervous about Saturday night, though. Carol had told me she was going to come over, so that I could get some "private" practice peeing in public. Contradiction in terms or not, if I was going to pee for Justin, I was going to have to get over my overwhelming trepidation about going in front of other people. I changed into a satin robe and laid one out on the bed for her. She arrived right after I'd finished curling my hair. I tried not to think about how beautiful she looked when she stripped and slipped into the bright-blue belted robe.

We sat on the couch, relaxing over glasses of white wine and soft music. Pretty soon Carol had pulled me up against her warm, full breasts, laughing and stroking my hair as I giggled and animatedly told her of my adventures during the week. Her fingertips had slipped inside the front of my robe and were gently stroking my belly. Eventually, I started fidgeting. She knew why. I blushed as she purposefully handed me a full glass of water and said, "Drink, sweetie."

By the time the glass was half empty, I was leaning hard against her, squirming and dutifully swallowing each time she raised the glass to my lips. She slipped her fingers inside my robe and trailed her fingers over my belly with a light, but still definite, pressure.

Finally I whispered, "I really have to go." My face was so hot I thought it was going to burst into flames.

"Are you sure, Amber?" As she spoke, Carol increased the pressure on her hand just the tiniest amount. I gasped and squeezed my legs together, shivering as I choked out, "Oooh, yes!"

"Very well, sweetie." She stood up, pulling me to my feet. "Let's go to the bathroom." Her voice was very calm and non-chalant, but my whole body trembled as I took her hand and let her lead me down the hall. She closed the bathroom door and turned the shower on. I clenched my legs together hard. Carol didn't look back as she tested the water and said, "Strip."

I nervously dropped my robe. She motioned me toward the shower.

"Stand in the water, but don't you dare go until I tell you to."

"Yes, ma'am," I whispered. I stepped in the shower, then suddenly crossed my legs, astonished to realize that I was so accustomed to going in the water now that I was really having to fight not to go.

"Kind of a surprise, isn't it?" She grinned, leaning back against the sink.

"Yes," I whispered, holding my legs together tightly.

"Do it," she said calmly. "Just the way you always do."

I carefully spread my legs, shivering as the water washed over my belly. I could feel my bladder getting ready to let go.

"You're not masturbating."

I squeezed my eyes shut, my face burning as I gingerly touched my finger to my clit. I wasn't going to rub. It was just too embarrassing. But then the first drops leaked out, and somehow, it just felt so right to rub while I peed. Then I didn't have any more time to think. I shivered again, releasing my control for just a moment. My bladder let loose and I groaned as my pee splashed out into the tub.

The sound of Carol's applause had me hiding my face in the shower spray. "Bravo, Amber. You're an excellent student."

"Um, thanks, I guess," I said with a blush, turning off the water and grabbing for my towel. I tugged, and looked up to see Carol holding onto the other end.

"You're welcome," she said firmly. With that, she took the towel and dried me off, thoroughly, rubbing vigorously between my legs while I blushed profusely. Then she dressed me in my robe, tied the belt, and led me by the hand back into the living room. Half a movie, another glass of wine, and two full glasses of water later, I was fidgeting like crazy again. Carol led me back to the bathroom. I stepped in the shower and closed my eyes, pressing my finger to my clit and concentrating hard on relaxing, waiting for her command. Suddenly, I felt her hand beneath mine. My eyes flew open to see her standing outside the open door, her beautiful naked breasts and neatly trimmed pubic hair shimmering with water spray.

"Pee, Amber," she ordered.

I stared at her, my mouth hanging open, as she purposefully slid her fingers between my labia. She leaned over and kissed my breast, ignoring the light splash of water on her face.

"I said, pee, Amber. Rub your clit and relax your bladder muscles. Now."

I stared, fascinated, as her tongue lapped over my areola. The tip hardened, as if it was reaching up for her touch. Her lips closed around my nipple and she sucked, long but deeply. As the sensation vibrated into my belly, my bladder let loose and I was peeing all over her hand. Her fingers held me open so that I could feel her touching inside my inner labia, feel her finger brushing my urethra as my urine gushed out. I came, shaking against her while she sucked my breast and played with my streaming pee.

I moaned, leaning hard against her. I was embarrassed to look at her, and too aroused to look away from where her lips were softly kissing my nipples and her fingers were still lightly caressing me.

"Let's go watch the end of the movie," she said with a smile. Trembling, I nodded. With both of us wearing just our towels, I let her lead me back into the living room to face another round of drinks.

This time, I lasted until the end of the video. I was shaking at the thought of what was going to happen. But the insistent touch of Carol's hands massaging my belly and the pressure in my bladder told me I was getting close. This time, Carol excused herself briefly before leading me back to the bathroom. When she drew me in, I was surprised to see a Water Pik hooked up to the sink next to it, the nozzle resting on the edge of the tub.

Carol turned the shower spray on very lightly, angling the head toward the middle of the tub. Then she turned on the flow to the Water Pik.

"I've adjusted the temperature," she said, peeling off her robe. This time, I let myself stare at her beautiful body. Her nipples were soft and full from the heat, her whole body slightly flushed above the small dark thatch between her legs. She climbed in the tub and sat down, then patted her thigh.

"Sit between my legs, Amber. You know what it feels like with my hands on you when you pee and when you climax. Now you're going to learn what it feels like when I make you come."

I was trembling when I dropped my robe and stepped into the soft spray of the shower. As I leaned back against her breasts, the shower hit right on my belly.

"Relax," she murmured, calmly and soothingly running her hands over my belly, pressing just enough to let me know she meant business. When I squirmed and arched back into her, her hand slid lower. I gasped as her fingers spread my pussy lips.

The water tickled over my pussy. With her other hand, Carol picked up the Water Pik and turned it on. At first, she directed the warm jet onto my belly. I gasped, arching up toward her.

"Not yet," she said, gradually moving the jet lower. "Stroke your breasts."

I moaned as jolts of sensation shot from my breasts to a spot deep inside my belly, teasing against my bladder. Each time I clenched my pussy muscles to hold back the pee, my cunt quivered. The jet moved lower, splashing over my labia. Then the water squirted over my clit. I gasped as waves of sensation washed through me.

"Now," Carol ordered. She held my labia open with her fingers, pressing firmly into my belly with the heel of her hand. As my bladder let loose, she directed the jet straight onto my clit. I screamed, bucking against her, the wonderful relief of peeing mixing into the orgasm exploding through my cunt. I collapsed into her arms, shaking.

"You're almost there, Beautiful," she whispered, nuzzling my neck as she directed the spray back onto my belly. The wonderful warm water washed over me, relaxing me to my bones as I snuggled back into her. "Tomorrow night, you're going to sit in the tub on Justin's cock. You're going to finger your breasts while he holds your pussy lips open and presses your belly with the palm of his hand and squirts the Water Pik jet over your clit. And when you climax, you're going to pee all over his hand and shaft while he comes up your cunt. Can you do that for me, Amber?"

"Oh, yes, ma'am," I whispered, whimpering as Carol once more peeled my labia open and directed the jet straight onto my clit. The climax rolled through me this time, long and low and shuddering, the last few drops leaking out of me as the tremors passed and I relaxed into her grip.

Carol kissed me softly on the neck. "Make me proud, Amber. My reputation's at stake here."

Monday morning, Justin called her at the crack of dawn to tell her her reputation was still unblemished. Then he made a fresh pitcher of juice, called in sick, and hauled me back into the shower.

Remembering

CELIA O'TOOLE

I lie here thinking of you, my cunt tingling with want. All of my attention is focused between my legs and I know that my desire has made my opening slippery to welcome you—or at least to welcome the thought of you.

I think of your cock and how it looked last night, firm and huge, rising erect from your lap as you sat on the bed, like a flagpole announcing your interest in me. The pink color of it was like a beacon, inviting me to lean over, lick it, suck it, taste its saltiness, and feel the velvety softness of its head. I remember the feel of your cock as it pushed against my pussy lips, spreading them with its swollen size, sliding through my slickness to ram its hardness into me. I remember how it felt to be filled by you, and to be fucked and fucked and fucked, the heat spreading through my insides like a golden glow, telling every cell it touched "You're OK. You're OK." I remember how your cock seemed to grow ever bigger, the pressure of your organ against the interior walls of my own a tight fit that seemed like a gift from heaven.

I remember how it felt as I rode you, as I screamed with ecstasy, how you grasped at my breasts, hungrily, as though fondling them was the greatest pleasure you'd ever felt. (What a gift you give to me when you take pleasure in my body!) I remember how you squeezed my breasts, pushed them together, made me feel sexy by creating cleavage from my A-cup breasts, stroked and pinched my nipples until they hardened and reached out to you. How, accepting their invitation, you took them into your mouth one by one and sucked and nipped, triggering wave after wave of orgasm in my already pulsating cunt.

I remember all this as I lie here listening to the sounds of children doing homework and preparing for bed. How I long for some privacy and a guarantee of an uninterrupted hour or two. I want to savor the memory of every moment we spent together, maybe not even to touch myself, but just to enjoy the arousal that the memory induces.

What would I do if I were alone? I imagine that I would remove my clothes and trace with my hands all the places that you touched. The sensations of my own hands on my skin—belly, breasts, cunt—would be enough to trigger climax after climax. And then the wanting would be overpowering and I'd have to be filled.

I'd retrieve the dildo from the closet shelf and touch its lifelike head to my clit. The cool temperature would be a shock at first, so I'd pull it away and try to warm it with my hands. But my throbbing cunt would have no patience for the warming process, so I'd put the dildo to my opening and push it in. The coldness of that silicone object would provide such a contrast to the warm, velvety firmness of your cock that I'd decide that hard fucking would be the only use for it. I'd grasp the molded base and shove it roughly up inside me, pounding it into me until I felt the squeezing of the deep contractions that only a cock—even if it's an artificial one—can induce. Then, I'd toss the toy aside and work my swollen pussy lips with my fingers, first firmly, then gently, then firmly again, bringing myself to orgasm after orgasm until I'd finally fall asleep.

But I'm not alone, and the demands of the children mean that I won't have an hour to myself anytime soon. One refuge remains, though, one moment of privacy that is respected even by the children. With a full bladder as an excuse, I steal off to the bathroom, my head still filled with images from last night. I pull off my jeans, then my panties, then fall against the bathroom wall as my hand finds my dripping cunt. I use the abundant slipperiness as lube and rub my fingers vigorously back and forth on my clit until the burning pleasure borders on pain. Then I plunge my fingers inside and fuck myself, biting my lip to avoid hollering out as I come, pulling up hard on my clit as the spasms begin to subside, triggering one more climax. Then a slow, gentle finger-fucking brings me down. I sit on the toilet and empty my bladder and come once again as I feel the flow of urine over my still-tingling pussy.

I can't wait to be alone with you again.

Bob & Carol & Ted (But Not Alice)

M Christian

"What are you afraid of?" Not spoken with scorn, with challenge though. This was Carol, after all. His Carol. The question was sweet, sincere—one lover to another: Really, honestly, what are you frightened of?

Robert fiddled with his glass of iced tea, gathering his thoughts. He trusted Carol—hell, he'd been happily married to her for five years so he'd better—but even so, it was a door he hadn't thought of opening in a long time.

They were sitting in their living room. A gentle rain tapped at the big glass doors to the patio, dancing on the pale blue surface of the pool beyond. In the big stone fireplace, a gentle fire licked at the glowing embers of a log.

Carol smiled—and, as always, when she did Bob felt himself sort of melt, deep inside. Carol...it shocked him sometimes how much he loved her, trusted her, loved to simply be with her. He counted himself so fortunate to have found the other half of himself in the tall, slim, brown-haired woman. They laughed at the same jokes, they appreciated the same kind of jazz, they both could eat endless platters of sashimi, and—in the bedroom, the garage, the kitchen, in the pool, car, and everywhere else the mood struck them—their lovemaking was always delightful, often spectacular.

"I don't know," Bob finally said, taking a long sip of his drink (needs more sugar, he thought absently). "I mean, I think about it sometimes—it's not as if I don't like what we do, but sometimes it crops up. A lot of the time it's hot, but other times it's kinda…fuck, disconcerting, you know. Like I should be thinking of what we're doing, what I want to do with you" —a sly smile there, hand on her thigh, kneading gently— "instead of thinking about, well, another guy."

Carol leaned forward, grazing her silken lips across his. As always, just that simple act—one glancing kiss—made his body, especially his cock, respond with desire. "Sweetie," she said, whispering hoarsely into his ear, "I don't mind. I think it's hot. I really do."

Bob smiled, flexing his jean-clad thighs to relish in his spontaneous stiffness. "I know—it just feels weird sometimes. I can't explain it."

"What do you think about? Talk to me about it—maybe that'll help a little bit." Her hand landed in his lap, curled around his shaft.

"Pretend I'm not here," she added, with a low laugh.

He responded with a matching chuckle. "Oh, yeah, right," he said, leaning forward to meet her lips. They stayed together, lips on lips, tongues dancing in hot mouths. Bob didn't know how to respond, so he just followed his instincts—his hand drifted up to cup Carol's firm, large breasts. Five years and she still had the power to reach down into his sexual self—to get to him at a cock-and-balls level. But there was something else.

"I think it's hot," Carol said again, breaking the kiss with a soft smack of moisture. "I think about it a lot, really. The thought of you with…what was his name again?"

Bob doubted Carol had really forgotten, but he smiled and played along. "Charley. College friend." Charley: brown curls, blue eyes, broad shoulders, football, basketball, geology, math, made a wicked margarita. Charley: late one night in their dorm room, both drunk on those wicked margaritas, Charley's hand on Bob's knee, then on his hard cock. "We fooled around for most of the semester, then his father died—left him the business. We stayed in touch for a year or so, then, well, drifted away. You know."

"I think it's wonderful," Carol said, smiling, laughing, but also tender, caring, knowing there was a Charley-shaped hole somewhere deep inside Bob. Carefully, slowly, she inched down the zipper on his shorts until the tent of his underwear was clearly visible, a small dot of pre-come marking the so-hard tip of his cock. "I think about it when we play—when we fuck."

Bob suspected, but hearing Carol say it added extra iron to his already throbbing hard-on. Carol normally wasn't one to talk during sex. This new, rough voice was even more of a turn-on.

Bob felt a glow start, deep down. Even to Carol, Charley was something private—but hearing Carol's voice, he felt as if he could, really, finally share it. "He was something else,

Charley was. Big guy, never would have thought it to look at him—that sounds stupid, doesn't it?"

Carol had gotten his shorts down, quickly followed by his underwear. Bob's cock had never seemed so big, so hard in his life. It was as if two parts of his life had met, with the force of both working to make him hard...so damned hard. Carol kissed the tip, carefully savoring the bead of come just starting to form again at the tip. "No, it doesn't. You're speaking from the heart, sexy—since when is anyone's heart logical or fair?"

He smiled down at her, taking a moment to playfully ruffle her hair before allowing himself to melt down into the sofa. "I wouldn't call him 'sweet' or 'nice'—but he could be, sometimes. He just liked...fuck," the words slipped from his mind as Carol opened her mouth and—at first—slowly, carefully started to suck on his cock. "Fuck...yeah, he liked life, I guess. I don't even think he thought of himself as gay or anything. He just liked to fuck, to suck, to get laid, you know. But it was special. I can't really explain it."

"You loved him, didn't you, at least a little bit?" Carol said, taking her lips off his cock for a moment to speak. As she did, she stroked him, each word a downward or upward stroke.

Bob didn't say anything, he just leaned back and closed his eyes. He knew she was right but that was one thing he wasn't quite willing to say—not yet. He'd come a long way, but that was still in the distance.

Carol smiled, sweetly, hotly, and dropped her mouth onto his cock again. This time her sucking, licking, stroking of his cock was faster, more earnest, and Bob could tell that she was aching to fuck, to climb on top of him and ride herself to a shattering, glorious orgasm. But she didn't. Instead, she kept sucking, kept stroking his cock, occasionally breaking into a whisper, then said, in a raw, hungry voice: "I think it's hot… not him just sucking your cock…but that you have had that. I bet sometimes…we look at the same guy…and want to know what he'd be like…to suck…to fuck."

Even though Bob was somewhere else, damned near where Carol wanted to be, he knew she was right. It was hot, it was special, and he recognized that. He wanted to haul her off her knees, get dressed, and bolt out the door to do just that. The kid who bagged their groceries sometimes at the Piggly Wiggly, that one linebacker, Russell Crowe: He wanted to take them home, rip off their shirts, lick their nipples, suck their cocks, suck their cocks, suck their cocks—

Then something went wrong. Just on the edge of orgasm, Carol stopped. Bob felt slapped, as if ice water had just been dumped into his lap. He opened his eyes and looked, goggle-eyed, as Carol got up off the floor, straightening her T-shirt over very hard nipples. "Didn't you hear that? Of all times for someone to ring the fucking doorbell."

. . .

Tugging up his pants, Bob rehearsed what he'd say: Mormon missionaries? Slam the door in their faces. Door-to-door salesman? The same. Someone needing directions? "Sorry, but you're way off," then do the same…

Just as Bob got to the door to the living room, he heard Carol—who'd been a lot more dressed to start with—saying, "Ted! How's it hanging?"

Bob rounded the corner, a smile already spreading across his face. Of all the people to have knocked on their front door, Ted was probably the only one who would have understood.

Ted and his charming wife, Alice, lived just across town. Normally, Bob and Carol would never in a million years have crossed paths with them—but it so happened that Ted worked in the coffee place right across the street from where Bob worked. After six months of going back and forth, Bob finally struck up a conversation with Ted and found out, much to his delight, that the tall, sandy-haired young man and he had a lot in common: the Denver Broncos, weekend sailing, and Russell Crowe movies. Bob and Carol felt very relaxed and even sometimes sexually playful around Ted and Alice, even going so far as to have a kind of sex party one night, when they all got way too wasted on tequila and some primo green bud that Ted had scored the night before. All they'd done was watch each other fuck, but it had been more than enough to blast Bob and Carol into happy, voyeuristic bliss—and to fuel their erotic fantasies for weeks afterward.

"Low and to the right," Ted answered, smiling wide and broad and planting a quick kiss on Carol's cheek. Bob gave Ted his own quick greeting—a full-body hug that only when he finished did Bob realize had probably given Ted more than he expected in regard to Bob's still rock-hard dick.

Bob and Carol smiled at each other, feeling relaxed and still playful in the presence of their friend. "Where's Alice at, Teddy? Somewhere in the depths of Colombia?" Bob said. Alice was the other half of Bean Seeing You, their little coffee-house, and was often away trying to wrangle up all kinds of stimulating delicacies—not all of them coffee-related.

"Worse than that," Ted said, playfully ruffling his friend's brown locks. "Nope: deepest, darkest Bakersfield. I'm kinda worried about her—the last expedition down there vanished without a trace."

Everyone laughing, more out of released tension than Ted's weird brand of humor, they retreated back to the living room and the couch. As Bob and Ted sprawled out on the couch while Carol got some drinks, Bob couldn't help but wonder if their friend had figured out that they'd been almost screwing their brains out a few minutes before. The thought of it made Bob grin wildly.

"Come on, bro," Ted said, picking up on the smile. "Out with it."

Suddenly tongue-tied, Bob was glad when Carol walked in with three tall, cool drinks. "One for the man of the house" —Bob—"one for the handsome stranger"—Ted—"and one for the horny housewife"—Carol. "Cheers!" she concluded, taking a hefty swallow of her own drink.

Bob and Ted toasted her, Bob almost coughing as he drank, the drinks being stiff, and then some. He smiled to himself again as he sank back into the sofa. Talking about Charley made him feel as if a secret had been released from some dark, compressed part of his mind. He felt light, airy, almost as though he was hovering over his body, looking down at Ted—tall, curly-haired, quick and bright Ted—and Carol: Carol, who even just thinking of made his body and mind think of their wonderful lovemaking.

Sneaking a furtive glance at Ted, Bob looked his friend over more carefully. In his new, unburdened vision, Ted looked...well, he wasn't like Charley, but there was still something about Ted that made Bob think of his college friend—no, his college lover. Something about their height, their insatiable appetite for life, their humor.

"Is it hot in here or is it just me?" Carol piped up, laughing at her own cliché. Bob and Ted laughed too—but then the sound dropped away to a compressed silence as Carol lifted off her T-shirt and theatrically mopped her brow.

Bob's mind bounced from Carol's beautiful breasts, and her obviously very erect nipples, to Ted's rapt attention on them. He was proud of Carol, proud that she was so lovely, so sexy. He wanted to reach out and grab her, pull her to him. He wanted to kiss her nipples as Ted watched. He wanted to sit her down on the couch, spread her strong thighs, and lick her cunt until she screamed, moaned, and held onto Bob's hair as orgasm after orgasm rocketed through her while Ted watched. He wanted to bend her over, slide his painfully hard cock into her, and then fuck her till she moaned and bucked against him as Ted watched. He wanted Ted....

Carol's shorts came off next. Naked, she stood in front of them. Like a goddess, she rocked back and forth, showing off her voluptuous form. But even though he loved her, and thought she was probably the most beautiful women he'd ever seen, Bob turned to look at Ted.

Ted, with the beautiful Carol standing right there in the room with him, was, instead, looking at Bob.

Bob felt his face grow flushed with...no, not with what

he expected. It wasn't embarrassment. Dimly, he was aware of Carol walking toward him, getting down on her hands and knees again, and, in a direct repeat of only minutes before, playfully tugging his cock out of his shorts and starting to suck on it.

Still watching Ted watching him, and Carol sucking his own cock, Bob smiled at him. In Carol's mouth, his cock jumped with a sudden influx of pure lust.

Carol, breaking her hungry relishing of his dick, said, "Bob, I really think Ted would like you to suck his cock."

Now Bob was embarrassed, but not enough to keep him from silently nodding agreement.

"I'd love that," Ted said, his voice low and rumbling. "I really would."

"Take your pants off, Ted," Carol said, stroking Bob's cock. "I want to watch."

Ted did, quickly shucking his shirt as well as his thread-bare jeans. He stood for a moment, letting Carol and Bob look at him. Bob had seen his friend's cock before, but for the first time he really looked at it. Ted was tall and thin, his chest bare and smooth. His cock was big—though maybe not as big as Bob's (a secret little smirk at that)—but handsome. It wasn't soft, but it also wasn't completely hard—but with Carol and Bob watching, Ted's cock grew firmer, harder, larger, until it stuck out from his lean frame at an urgent, 45-degree angle.

"Bob…" Carol said, her voice purring with lust, "…suck Ted's cock. Please, suck it."

Ted crawled up on the sofa, lying down so that his head was on one armrest, his cock sticking straight up. His eyes were half-closed, and a sweet, sexy smile played on his lips.

Bob reached down, turning just enough to reach his friend and not dislodge Carol from her earnest sucking of his dick, and gently took hold of Ted's cock. It was warm, almost hot, and slightly slick with a fine sheen of sweat. He could have looked at it for hours, days, but with Carol working hard on his own dick, he felt his pulse racing, his own hunger beating hard in his heart.

At first he just kissed it, tasting salty pre-come. With a flash of worry that he wouldn't be good, first he licked the tip, exploring the shape of the head with his lips and then his tongue. As his heart hammered heavier and his own cock pulsed with sensation, he finally took the head into his mouth and gently sucked and licked. Ted, bless him, gave wonderful feedback—gently moaning and bucking his slim hips just enough to let Bob know that he was doing a good job.

As Carol worked him, he worked Ted. They were a long train of pleasure, a circuit of moans and sighs. Time seemed to stretch, distance to compress, until the whole world was just Ted's dick in Bob's mouth, Bob's dick in Carol's mouth—all on that wonderful afternoon.

Then, before he was even aware it was happening, Bob felt his orgasm pushing, heavy and wonderfully leaden: down through his body, down through his balls, down through his cock, and—in a spasming orgasm that made him break his earnest sucking of Ted's cock—to moan, sigh, almost scream with pleasure. Smiling at his friend, Ted followed quickly behind, with only a few quick jerks of his cock as Bob rested his head on Ted's knee.

Bob felt… *good,* like something important, magical, and special had happened. The world had grown, by just a little bit, but in a very special way. Resting against his friend's knee, Carol kissing his belly, he smiled. Everything was all right with the world.

· · ·

Later, the sun set, and as everyone was very much exhausted by many more hours of play, Ted stumbled to the front door, Carol helping him navigate through the dim house. "Thanks for coming," she said with a sweet coo, almost a whisper, so as not to wake the heavily slumbering Bob in the next room. She kissed him, soft and sweet, smiling to herself at the variety of tastes on his lips.

"I was happy to—very. Thanks for asking me to…come," Ted said, smiling, as he opened the front door.

Carol smiled. "Thank you for giving him such a wonderful gift. Next weekend then?"

"Definitely. Next time I'll bring Alice."

Another gentle kiss, a mutual "Good-night," and the door closed.

Getting Dirty
ERICA DUMAS

I can smell the bay, a foggy breeze coming up 16th Street at my heels. I'm dressed to kill: tight blue PVC shorts and a red top, just like every stereotype of a whore in any Hollywood movie. And I'm a real whore tonight, a whore with a heart of gold.

I turn off onto Capp Street, bathed in yellow sodium light to match the stink of human urine. If this was the 1st or the 15th of the month, it would be hopping, but tonight it's relatively quiet. I hear the car coming up behind me, and a shiver runs up my spine. I turn, step off the curb into the alley, and look at the driver, waving, my best whore-smile pasted on my face. It's a businessman, his tie undone, his suit rumpled. Maybe coming from the strip clubs in North Beach, finding himself too horny to go home without some satisfaction. I feel a shudder of relief and disappointment as he goes past, his eyes studiously avoiding me. I take a deep breath, smelling ammonia and dead pigeons. I step back onto the sidewalk and hear a shout from the empty lot. "Hey, hooker! You want some action, whore?" I squint my eyes: Five or six young men, white and Latino, drinking from paper bags. One of them gets up to walk toward me, making kissing noises. I feel the cold grip of fear. That's when I hear the shout from behind me—rude and insistent.

"Damn, now that's what I like to see for sale!"

I turn, bending down to peer in the window of the Jaguar. I see you, your dark eyes invisible in the shadows. I pray my voice doesn't shake as I smile and ask you: "Want a date?"

"How much?" The youths are all up, now, shuffling slowly as if waiting for you to go before they surround me. I want to name a figure as low as possible so that you'll accept, give me a chance to get out of here.

"Eighty bucks," I say. "Full service." This time my voice *is* shaking, for real.

You laugh. "Too much."

"It's only fifty for a blowjob," I tell you, glancing over my shoulder, trying not to look as if I'm glancing over my shoulder.

"Too much," you repeat. You hit the button and the window starts rolling up with a dull hum.

They're all shouting, crowding up behind me, now. One of them reaches out and grabs my waist, saying, "Don't go with the gringo, baby, come home with me!" I can feel his crotch grinding against my ass, his cock hard in his pants. Another one starts rubbing his crotch and leans in toward me, one hand against the car. His cock's hard as well. My heart is pounding, my throat constricting with terror. I tell myself there's no way you're going to leave me; I know you care too much to just ditch me like this. Pulling away from the other men, I bend over toward your window. In one smooth motion, I pull up my shirt, smile, and wink at you.

"Make me an offer," I say, watching your eyes caress my tits. The boys are hooting and hollering, groping me, saying, "Come on, man, just keep driving, we'll take care of her!" and "Don't you know better than to mess with whores?" and "Yeah, baby, show him your tits, that'll convince him!" I feel the first one's cock against my ass as I bend down further to let you see my tits better. "Make me an offer," I beg, pinching my nipples.

"I'll give you twenty-five for full service," I hear you say, your voice aggressive, demanding, and I know there's no negotiating, which is what makes me say, "Thirty." You shake your head. "For thirty bucks I want it all," you say, and I see the window go up, feel the hot bodies against mine as fear stabs through me. I push myself up against the car door as I hear the elated shouts around me, feel a pair of hands on my bare breasts, and now I'm pulling away from them and pushing my breasts up against the cold glass of the window, feeling the nipples harden against the smooth surface even as one of the hands around me starts to unzip my hotpants.

I'm so scared when I feel them undressing me that for an instant I think I'm going to wet my pants, as if they weren't wet already. You just keep driving. My voice cracks as I shriek out: "All right, thirty—thirty for around-the-world," but you don't stop, and I shout, "Twenty-five! Twenty-five," and you flip me off. I'm desperate, terrified, feeling hands down my pants and rubbing hard between my legs, fingers pressing the thin PVC deep between my lips, and once they get that zipper down there won't be any PVC between their fingers and my crotch. I feel lips kissing my legs, hot breath and tongue on the back of my neck, fingers pinching my exposed nipples, hands tangling in my long hair. I'm desperate, tears of terror forming in my eyes, but you don't even look up at me until I scream, "All right, twenty! Twenty bucks! Twenty bucks for everything, around the world for twenty dollars, mister, and I got a real nice back door!" You brake, look at me as I pull my top back up, glance around to see all the faces and hands swirling around me. You cock your head toward the Jag's passenger door. "Fuck off!" I shout to the guys all around me, pushing them back, shoving their hands off me, kicking and spitting, grabbing wrists and twisting to get them out of my hair. I get away, scurry around the back of the car. I hear the disappointed shouts, curses in Spanish and English. I realize I should have gone around the front of your car; what if you change your mind and decide to drive off all of a sudden? I know there's no chance of that, but it all seems so real I can almost believe you would.

The door lock goes popping up; I yank the door open and get in as the guys crowd around. They don't try to stop the car; you floor it and I see their upthrust fingers in the side mirror as I pull my top back down, my hands shaking. I look over at you and smile nervously, feeling my stomach melt as you give me that cruel, heartless look I so rarely get. I can really believe that you don't care that you almost got me raped— and do I really know any better? "What's your name?" I ask.

"Jake," you tell me, and I love that. It's the name you use when we're playing together, when you have to be the sort of bastard I so want you to be. "How old are you?"

"Twenty-three," I say, cleanly shaving ten years. Not because I need to be young, but because any street whore would probably bullshit you.

You snort in disgust. "Yeah, right. How old are you really?"

"All right," I say, smiling. "Nineteen." Not the answer you were expecting, but you just smile grimly.

"I'm Cassie," I tell you. "It was twenty-five, right? For full service?"

"Twenty. For around the world," you growl, and I feel a quiver inside me that tells me you're not taking any shit. "And I hear you got a real nice back door."

I smile. "Oh, yeah, that's right. Twenty."

"Reach in my front pocket," you tell me.

I smile and reach into the pocket of your scratchy wool pants. There's a small roll of bills in there, and the feel of it in my hand gives me a surge of pleasure. I take it out and my heart sinks. I count out two crumpled twenties.

"Put one back," you say.

I hold it out for you; you snatch it and stuff it in your shirt pocket. I scowl at you but tuck the single bill into my boot.

Then I brighten, knowing it's time to start really working. "Where do you want to go? I know a parking lot that's good, over on Harrison. Or we could always park and get a room, if you want to pay for a whole hour—that'd be another twenty dollars."

"I don't need an hour," you tell me, and then say, "Twin Peaks" as you turn right on 18th Street.

"There's a lot of cops up there," I say.

"They won't mess around with us," you answer. "I've always wanted to take a whore up there."

"I'd like that," I say, and that's what I am: your whore, being taken up to Twin Peaks so that you can use me, around-the-world, use every part of me for twenty bucks. In my real life, I bill at two-forty an hour, and I spend all those hours with my clothes on except when I'm reading briefs in the bathtub.

You growl at me: "You don't kiss, do you?"

"Kiss?"

"On the lips."

"If you want to," I say coquettishly.

"I don't want you to kiss me. I know where that mouth's been."

"All right," I say. "I don't have to kiss you. It's easier that way, anyway."

"Good. And don't talk too much."

I lean against you and let my hand drop into your lap, gently massaging your crotch as I take a deep breath and smell your sweat. I don't have my seat belt on—another turn-on. I haven't ridden without my seat belt since I was sixteen. I feel you getting hard against my palm. I lean harder and press my cheek against the bulge in your pants. I start to kiss your hard cock through your pants.

"Don't take it out while I'm driving," you say as I feel the car tipping and turning. We're mounting the hill, the Jag's suspension taking the curves and potholes effortlessly as you drive much too fast.

"Don't worry," I say. "I just want to kiss it a little. Through your pants."

But I don't just want to kiss it through your pants; I want to take it out and gulp it down, and I can feel myself getting wet under my tight PVC pants, my juices slicking up the smooth inside of them since I'm not wearing any panties. I rub my hand over your cock and inhale deeply, smelling you and loving it with all my being.

We reach the summit. You put the Jag in park and pull the emergency brake. I sit up and look out at the city, at the million bright lights diffused by the ether of the fog like fairy dust lit by a blowtorch.

"It's so beautiful up here," I say. "It's gorgeous."

Which is when I feel your hand snaking through my hair, pushing me down roughly. Just like in my fantasy, the fantasy I've related to you more times than there are lights in San Francisco. You push my face into your crotch and I don't need to be told twice. I fumble with your belt and unzip your pants. Your cock is hard and sweaty, unwashed after a long day at the office. I smell the sharpness of your pre-come, the muskiness of your crotch, and I know exactly how it will taste.

I part my lips, take a deep breath, and gulp you all the way down in one smooth movement, deep-throating your cock as if I've been practicing on it for years, which I have. I feel my lips tickled by your pubic hair, hold my breath as long as I can, then come up for air and lick your head all over. You grunt softly, your hand still tangled in my hair, guiding me up and down as I suck you. I lick up and down the shaft, tease your balls out of your jockey shorts to lick them. You pull me back up to the top of your cock, your other hand guiding it into position. You push me down, almost choking me as I swallow you. I stay down even longer this time, seeing stars before you let me up to lick your head and pump your shaft with my spit-slick hand.

I look up at you, my eyes wide. I talk like a whore, or at least like all the whores do in my world. "You like that, baby? I love sucking your cock. You've got such a nice big cock." Then you grip my hair and I take you down again, feeling your smooth shaft glide up my wide-open throat. When I come up I rub you all over my face and feel the spittle cooling my cheeks.

"That pussy any better than that mouth?"

"It's real nice," I smile up at you. "Want to try it?"

"You're not going to give me any shit about how I have to use a condom, are you?"

My stomach churns as I think about the feeling of your naked cock in my pussy, seeming so new as I contemplate it. "Not if you don't want to," I say cheerfully.

"Then yeah, I'll try it. Get those shorts off," you say.

I squirm on the plush seat of the Jag, unzipping the zippers in the front and the back of the kinky little garment, then snug them down over my hips and wriggle out of them. I'm not wearing anything underneath, anything at all, and my pussy's as slick with sweat under the sticky PVC as it is with the juice of my arousal. I lean back in the seat and spread my legs, fingering my pussy, feeling a lightning bolt of pleasure shoot up my spine as I slide one finger in.

"How d'ya want me? Front seat or back? You want me doggy style? I love to be fucked doggy style."

You reach over me and pop my seat while pushing back on my chest; I go flat on my back in an instant, and you scramble over me and position yourself between my legs. You don't even give me the slightest warmup—whores aren't supposed to need foreplay. I spread wide and moan softly as I feel the head of your cock against my pussy. It slides in effortlessly, bringing a gasp from me as the head of your cock hits my cervix, jarring me but making me grind my hips up against you. I reach my hands down into your pants and cup your buttocks as I feel them flex with exertion as you begin to fuck me. Your cock feels so familiar yet so unfamiliar sliding into my whore's pussy, and I'm so close to my orgasm I'm afraid I'll come too soon and spoil the illusion. Whores aren't supposed to enjoy it *this* much, are they?

I'm cooing into your ear as I lick your salty neck, as your hot breath caresses my bare shoulders with each grunt. "Oh, yeah, baby, I love that. I love that so much. This is my favorite position, baby."

"I thought you said you liked doggy style," you say.

"I like that one, too."

"Then get on your knees."

"It's easier in the back seat."

You pull yourself off me and lean back. "Go ahead. What was your name again."

"It's Cassie, Jake."

You don't seem impressed that I remembered your name. You nod toward the back seat, and I climb over and get on my hands and knees. "What if the cops come by?" I ask.

"Don't worry about it," you say, and get into the back seat behind me, your hips pressing up against my naked ass. It's incredibly cramped in here, and you have to lean forward to keep from hitting your head on the roof of the car, which makes you press your body against mine, and the heat excites me.

You enter me in one smooth thrust again, my pussy feeling tighter in this position, your cock feeling bigger. I moan as I rock back and forth in time with your thrusts; I'm incredibly close, now. Your hips pump against me, driving your cock harder and harder into me with each thrust. I feel your body slapping against my thighs, your fingernails digging into the flesh of my ass. I want to say something dirty, filthy, but I can't speak; I'm tottering on the brink of orgasm.

"You're really wet," you growl. "You're getting off on this, aren't you? You love being fucked like this, don't you?"

"Yeah," I manage to gasp. "I love your cock. You're going to make me come, baby. I'm going to come for you, Jake. You like it when your whores come for you?"

"Can you come with a cock in your ass?"

I stop moving, only half-feigning the shock and strain in my voice. "N-no. I mean, I never have." And yet, I remember what I promised you, and the knowledge that you're taking me there sends another surge into my pussy, making my muscles clench around your cock. "Wh-what do you mean?"

"You said around the world."

"Yeah, but—"

You pull out of me, move up slightly, lean heavily on my body to get your cock into position as you pry open my cheeks with your thumbs. I feel the head of your cock pressing against my puckered anus as you begin to work it in. Your cock is so wet with my juices—but that's not why it pops in so easily, making me gasp and almost sob in terrified pleasure. I'm so unused to being entered there; the sensation of your cock sliding in makes my stomach go all liquid, makes my body shudder as I mount toward orgasm. But none of that is why it slides in so easily; the lubricating suppository I inserted earlier makes my ass slick and open, ready and willing to take your cock. That's why, as I feel your balls snuggling up against my ass cheeks, I feel the first spasms of my climax beginning, even as I push back against you hard, forcing your cock into me as deeply as it will go. Then you're pumping, too, and I'm coming harder, riding the wave of orgasm, feeling you fuck me there, in my darkest spot, grunting, "Come on, take it, Cassie" as you thrust into me, as you suddenly go rigid and I feel your cock pulsing in my tight hole, just as, totally unexpectedly, I reach my second orgasm and come on your pumping cock. As you fill me full of your essence.

"Oh, yeah," I moan hoarsely. "Your cock is so good, Jake."

You just lie on top of me for a minute, breathing hard into my ear, your breath hot on me. I reach back and caress your face.

"That was so good," I whisper. "Did you like that, Jake?"

"I'll take you back down," you say, and reach down to zip up. I lie there on my belly still feeling you inside me, feeling my ass slick with lube and your come. This is part of it, for me—being used and then discarded, no strings, no attachments. No matter how many years we've been together, you know just how to abandon me.

You buckle your belt, climb into the driver's seat, and start the car. As we twist down the Twin Peaks curves, I struggle into the front seat.

"Don't get come on the upholstery," you tell me. "My wife rides in this car."

I almost can't resist laughing, but I manage to suppress the urge. I turn onto my side so as not to rub my lube-and-come-slicked crack against the seat, and I wriggle back into the skintight PVC shorts. Now it feels *really* wet in there, my pussy mingled with your come mingled with lube. I zip up and buckle the little belt just as you turn onto 18th Street.

"Same place OK?"

"Take me up to 16th," I tell you. "There's more action up there this time of night."

"All right. Capp?"

"Make it Mission. Right here's just fine."

You pull up to the curb. "Thanks," I say.

And you don't thank me; you just say, "See you" as if it was nothing.

I get out of the car. By now it's two o-clock in the morning, and the last thing I want to do is be alone on these streets. Lucky thing the parking garage is right here.

I look around one last time, remembering all the nights when, coming back from an expensive dinner in the Castro or Noe Valley, you and I took a little detour and drove past this low-rent red-light district, me craning my head to get a better look and you chuckling, knowing the surge of fantasy that was going through my body and mind at the moment I saw the tawdry hookers parading their wares to the passing cars. I remember how you would reach over and slip your hand between my thighs, stroke my pussy through my jeans or under my skirt. How you would tell me how wet I was, how some day you were going to turn me out onto Capp Street. And that night was tonight—finally, like the sudden realization of every fantasy I've ever had, every sex dream I've ever confessed to you.

The Latino parking attendant eyes me suspiciously, his eyes devouring me with everything he's got.

"Busy night?" he asks as I give him the ticket. The side of his mouth twists in a smile.

"I'll say," I tell him.

"That'll be twenty dollars."

I can't help but smirk as I bend down and take the crumpled bill out of my black knee-high boot. I hand him the money; he hands me my exit ticket.

"Take it easy," he tells me, and I blow him a kiss.

As I mount the onramp to the bridge, the Lexus ticking and purring, I try not to speed; I want you to get home before I do, so that you're showered and clean, scrubbed rosy and lying in bed, maybe even thinking about me, your cock hard when I walk in still dirty from my walk on the wild side, my mouth watering to taste how clean your cock is.

Because then I'll get to make you dirty all over again. Just the way I like you. Though I doubt you'll ever be as dirty as me.

Into the Labyrinth

XAVIER ACTON

I love five things about Club Labyrinth.

First is the club it's held in, with its dozens of corridors leading nowhere, its many shaded crevasses and poorly lit booths where you're lucky if the black-garbed cocktail waitress or latex-clad Peachy Puff girl—usually a cross-dressed guy— even bothers to tell you not to smoke, let alone to stop necking (and she never takes your order).

Second is the music they play, all dark-trance with a fetish edge, grinding rhythms mingled with moans and cheesy propositions. For me it's raw sex distilled into the most bewitching kind of rock 'n' roll. If you were going to be sarcastic you might tease me that it reminds me of my youth, which maybe wasn't that long ago but still seems a distant memory— except when I'm hanging out at Labyrinth.

Third is the smell, if you can believe that—incense and

cigarettes, whiskey and bodies, musk and wine. Any other place, any other time, the cocktail of odors would sicken me, but there's something special about the way that dark maze stinks that evokes the adventurer in me.

Fourth, and here we're getting to the good part, is the way the women dress, or is that *girls?* They seem like girls to me, I guess, but most of them have been of legal drinking age for long enough to see a president come and go, so let's call them women for the sake of argument. The place has a dress code, one of the only clubs in the city that has one and actually enforces it. Man or woman, you're not getting through that door if you're not wearing some sort of leather, latex, or PVC—and not just on your feet. Chain mail and pirate shirts will get you laughed at and sent sulking back to your car. As a result, the women there are clad without exception in materials natural or synthetic—but very, very kinky…high leather boots, shimmering black latex bustiers, barely legal miniskirts, glittery silver tights. Let's take Katrina, for instance: That night when the really interesting stuff started to happen, she was wearing black patent leather hotpants and a matching, skin-hugging bustier that defied gravity the way it stayed on her. Her dyed-black hair was teased into a voluptuous mane, and her tongue piercing flashed whenever she spoke.

The men are dressed similarly, if less flamboyantly, as I was this particularly night when the really interesting stuff started to happen—in PVC pants, knee-high boots, and a low-cut latex tank top. It was steamy as hell as I danced up behind Vanessa, and the sweat that slicked up the contact of her bare back and my upper chest wasn't a result of just the dancing or the temperature of the smoke-laden air.

Because that's the fifth and final thing I love about Labyrinth: Vanessa. She loves dancing on a floor full of freaks like she loves nothing else in this world. And she loves teasing me while she's doing it, knowing I can't take my eyes off her. And knowing I can't take my eyes off how close she's dancing to Katrina. Who had been flirting with her for weeks, while I watched, wondering if it would go anywhere. And knowing, that night, that it was about to.

• • •

Perhaps I'd started the whole thing, acknowledging to Vanessa that I thought Katrina was hot after that first night we'd chatted at Labyrinth, about the tighter-than-tight Hello Kitty shirt Katrina had been wearing—no bra—and the Pochacco lunchbox Vanessa was carrying. Any comments I'd made in the past about that lunchbox being a vaguely undignified accoutrement for a woman of thirty simply vanished into thin air when I saw Katrina coveting the damn thing. She and Vanessa made eye contact for half an hour as they traded lipstick, shopping tips, phone numbers. Vanessa teased me that she wasn't going to call Katrina, just to get back at me for drooling over her so much. Until I pointed out that Vanessa had been drooling even more than me. "Yeah," she finally admitted. "I guess I was."

But still she didn't call, claiming shyness, which was the silliest thing I had ever heard. Vanessa wasn't shy—maybe she was only busy, or maybe she was a little uncomfortable with how much I'd liked Katrina. Which was silly, too, because if there's a woman who could truly turn my head away from Vanessa, I certainly haven't encountered her yet. But I didn't push the issue, didn't remind Vanessa that she still had Katrina's phone number. And there things stood: a vivid fantasy of mine, Katrina and Vanessa making out on the dance floor at Labyrinth.

Until the three of us bumped up together on that very same dance floor, a few weeks later. And I knew somehow that this time there would be nothing left to my imagination.

• • •

Katrina and Vanessa didn't talk. Neither one bore cartoon characters, so maybe there was nothing to talk about—and the music was far, far too loud out there, anyway. Instead, they made eye contact, and as they ground closer and closer in time with the music, Vanessa wriggled her body like a stripper. I expected Katrina to back away, but she didn't. Instead, their slow dance continued until they made contact, their bodies against each other, Vanessa's bare belly touching Katrina's as their hips synchronized perfectly in a split second, as I hovered back a foot or so, watching incredulously.

And that's when Katrina, who for all I knew didn't even have a last name, kissed my wife.

• • •

It wasn't one of those "girl–girl" kisses, either. It was hard and hot, mouths open, teeth grinding as Vanessa gnawed on Katrina's lower lip, the way she likes to do to me. That's one thing about Vanessa: It's all teeth and tongue when she kisses you, as if she's a tiger left alone with her meal, never mind that it's still alive. I saw Katrina reacting, her arms snaking around Vanessa, pulling her close as she parted her legs slightly and as Vanessa let her thigh slip between them. They kissed hungrily, and I felt myself getting hard in my skintight PVC. I backed off another step, suddenly feeling superfluous, as the second most beautiful woman in the world kissed the most beautiful. At that instant, I just wanted to watch.

Which is what everyone else on the dance floor apparently wanted to do, too; I could feel the eyes all around, drinking in the scene of my wife kissing a beautiful stranger, their half-exposed bodies grinding together in time with Miranda Sex Garden.

I was about to pull back farther, not wanting to disrupt the gorgeous scene, when suddenly I felt a hand on my belt.

It was Vanessa, reaching back to grab me and pull me in. Which would have been a little less convincing if at that moment I hadn't felt a second hand, this one gloved in lace, caressing my cheek, sliding into my longish hair and pulling me.

It was Katrina: Like synchronized swimmers, the two women pulled me hard into their scene, my hard cock meeting Vanessa's ass, her pert cheeks smooth and inviting through her short latex skirt.

And Katrina, breaking her lip-lock with my wife, pressed her lovely lips to mine, and I felt her silver-spiked tongue caressing mine, coaxing me in further. And when her lips left mine, Vanessa's were there to replace them, as Katrina began kissing Vanessa's neck.

"Is this all right?" I shouted over the music, so overwhelmed by the sudden realization of my fantasy that I couldn't believe it was actually happening, or that it was actually OK.

"That depends," Vanessa shouted back. "Is it all right with you?"

"Definitely," I yelled.

"What?"

And I kissed her, hard, telling her all she needed to know. Katrina's tongue was flickering into Vanessa's ear, teasing it. And eyes all around were watching us, some jealous, some fascinated, some turned on.

"Let's get private," shouted Vanessa.

"Where?"

"In public," she answered, and took my hand and Katrina's, tugging us along. Katrina laughed, leaned toward me, and kissed me on the lips as Vanessa dragged us off the dance floor and down one of the many corridors of the club.

We'd acquired an entourage, but as Vanessa led us through the depths of the darkness we lost them all. When she'd found the hallowed kiosk she'd been looking for, she dragged us in. It was a little corner, one so far back that almost no one ever stumbled in even though it was complete with a garish, lime-green couch from some hellish thrift store. The funny thing is, though, I'd never seen anyone so much as making out on the thing. This time I knew that wouldn't be the case.

Vanessa guided Katrina onto the couch, then climbed on top of her and pulled me down. We made a sandwich, the two women making out as Vanessa quickly unzipped Katrina's bustier. She had small, firm breasts with pierced nipples. Vanessa began to kiss Katrina's breasts and ground her ass against back my crotch. Her knee came to rest between Katrina's legs, pushing hard into her crotch so that Katrina moaned. Vanessa was a good three or four inches shorter than Katrina, a good eight inches shorter than me, so she fit perfectly between us, my mouth kissing the back of Vanessa's neck—one of her favorite things—while I watched her tonguing a beautiful pair of breasts.

Then I felt one of Katrina's hands slipping between my legs, caressing my cock, as she grabbed my hair with her other hand and pulled me down to kiss her.

If I hadn't already been hard, I would have been. I felt Katrina's open palm gently squeezing my balls, moving up to press against my hard shaft through the tight pants. She began to unzip my pants.

We've always been ostensibly nonmonogamous, Vanessa and I, but it had literally been years since I'd felt another woman's hand on my cock. There was a different texture to it, a different way Katrina gripped me—more tentative, perhaps, than Vanessa's sure hand, but equally exciting. Katrina and I kissed hard, our tongues mingling, Vanessa's body curled neatly between us, Vanessa's mouth on Katrina's nipple, sucking. I moaned as Katrina began to slowly jack me off.

"People are watching," she said when our lips parted for an instant.

I glanced over my shoulder and saw two or three club-goers watching us, fascinated, trying to look nonchalant. When I looked back at them, they scattered. Then Katrina was pulling on my hair again, twisting my face insistently around, pressing her lips to mine, kissing me. God, her mouth tasted good—clove cigarettes and Jack Daniels. She let go of my hair so that she could let her hands gently snake down Vanessa's back, curving over her ass—until they reached the hem of her short skirt.

And pulled it up.

I guess it shouldn't have surprised me that Vanessa wasn't wearing anything under there; if she hadn't planned the whole thing on the phone with Katrina, it just couldn't have gone so smoothly. And in this age of safe sex, how could Katrina, who seemed like a vaguely responsible girl, have known that Vanessa and I don't use condoms with each other?

Which she must have known, from the sure way she reached up, took my cock in her hand, and guided it between Vanessa's spread thighs.

I'll give her this, too: She gently parted Vanessa's lips with her fingers, sliding one fingertip into my wife's pussy to make sure she was sufficiently lubricated. And she certainly was—more lubricated than I had felt her in months, which I discovered as soon as my cockhead found her familiar entrance. I thrust forward, my cock sinking smoothly into Vanessa as her back arched and she moaned. Which is when Vanessa hoisted herself more fully onto her hands and knees— giving Katrina the room she needed to pull up Vanessa's shirt, and start caressing my wife's breasts with her tongue.

All the while, I could feel Katrina's hand against the base of my cock, against my balls as she rubbed Vanessa's clit with her thumb. That's usually all it takes to get Vanessa off during intercourse, and while I knew it well, I had never felt another woman's hand doing it while I fucked Vanessa. Which was enough of a thrill to drive me toward my own orgasm, but not before Vanessa's arms curled around Katrina's head, gripping her close as I felt the first spasms begin in Vanessa's cunt.

She didn't utter a cry, or maybe I just couldn't hear it over the music. She only shuddered, and her pussy spasmed again, and again, and again as I felt my climax coming as I thrust faster and faster into my wife. And then I threw back my head, feeling droplets of sweat scatter all about me, and I came harder than I'd come in as long as I could remember. Gasping, I felt my cock squeezing deep inside Vanessa's tightened pussy. I felt Katrina's hand caressing my balls and the shaft of my penis, coaxing the last droplets of come out of me.

Katrina hoisted herself back up to the head of the couch so that she could kiss Vanessa deeply. Then she locked eyes with me, and I knew what she wanted. I leaned forward and kissed her, hungry for her taste and thankful for her indulgence. But if anyone was indulging anyone, it remained to be seen.

I caught a blaze of light out of my peripheral vision, turned my head, and was inexorably blinded.

"Bouncer," shouted Katrina, and started giggling. The bouncer dropped the flashlight, locked eyes with me in a way I like to think Katrina never would have. He was a big, beefy guy with a goatee and a Psychic TV tattoo on the back of his hand. My eyes dazzled, I saw him only as a silhouette as he made an obvious movement—pointing toward the exit.

Thrown out of a fetish club: long one of my fantasies. I zipped up, climbed off Vanessa, and helped her to her feet.

Katrina pulled her top back on and Vanessa yanked her shirt down. The bouncer was still standing there, not saying a word, tapping his booted foot impatiently.

Vanessa and I, as one, like synchronized swimmers, turned to Katrina. As if we'd choreographed the whole thing beforehand, we made the same gesture the bouncer had: a distinct indication of the door. But this time, our eyebrows were raised.

A smile broke across Katrina's face, and she nodded mischievously as the bouncer stepped up behind me.

The three of us didn't let the door hit us in the ass on the way out.

The Last Train

P. E. BRINK

Why did I let myself get talked into this? Alex wondered. It was late at night, and he was riding the last train of the evening.

He sat on a hard orange subway seat, facing forward in the open square of seats next to the door. The motion of the moving train pulled him comfortably backward.

On the other side of the entrance was Jack, on one of the pairs of seats that faced sideways. Jack was dressed in the same postwork uniform as he was: slacks, white dress-shirt, top button unbuttoned where the tie had been. Jack had dark hair, a slightly bent nose, too much eyebrow. Alex worked out with Jack twice a week. He's well built, thought Alex, with a brief pang of envy until he remembered that he, too, had added some muscle. Then his eyes took in the girl, and the envy returned with a vengeance.

Sitting next to Jack, on the seat between Jack and the

entrance, a beautiful and young-looking girl sat with one leg casually draped over one of Jack's legs. Her blonde hair was done in a ponytail, and she wore a white crop top that exposed her bellybutton. The outlines of her bra were clearly visible. Her breasts were on the small side, but sufficient to pull the hem of the top away from her body, leaving it not quite in contact with her stomach. She wore a short beige skirt that showed off long thin legs, white socks that barely rose above the ankle, and shiny patent black mary janes. She looked, thought Alex, about sixteen. Only a careful study of her long legs and face, with the slight signs of maturity there, would allow an observer to guess her true age, which Alex knew was twenty-nine.

Her name was Tori, short for Victoria. *My wife,* thought Alex. Tori and Jack exchanged a kiss. Jack had asked Tori to dress up this way. He had said it would enhance the atmosphere of adventure.

Alex watched as Jack placed his hand on Tori's thigh just where her skirt ended. I agreed to all this, Alex dimly remembered. Jack had chosen his seat for him, and he had agreed not to move until the last stop. "Sit there, pretend you don't know us," Jack had said. Tori removed her leg from its awkward position over Jack's knee, but did nothing about the hand.

Tori had agreed to everything, too. In fact, she had looked more than a little enthusiastic. Which was when Alex first started to wonder whether the whole "adventure" was such a good idea.

Jack put his arm around Tori, his hand hooking under her shoulder on the other side, two of his fingers resting against the side of Tori's left breast.

Jack stroked up and down Tori's thigh, just slightly to the inside. They kissed again.

They're pretending they don't know me, either, Alex thought. Pretending all too well.

The train stopped, the doors opened. Jack's hand came to rest on Tori's knee. Tori smiled at him. A slightly hunched, well-dressed black lady with gray hair came in and took a seat. She sat in the second row of seats behind the couple, facing Alex. Since she was on the same side of the aisle as Jack and Tori, the seats in front of her might possibly obstruct her view of them. It was hard to tell for sure, from where Alex was sitting.

The train started moving again. Tori put her leg back over Jack's knee. There was a section of train, directly across the aisle from Jack and Tori, that had a view of Tori's panties, which Alex had understood were to be pink cotton. Alex wished he was sitting in one of those privileged seats, but they lay vacant.

Jack whispered something into Tori's ear, and she smiled at him and nodded. Alex couldn't hear what he said. His ears burned.

They stayed like that, her leg over his knee, for another stop. The door opened. *Someone boarding the train will see her panties,* thought Alex. But no one boarded.

Tori looked vaguely disappointed. She tilted her head up to whisper something to Jack. He smiled. The arm that was wrapped around Tori slipped down a little, then rose. In the process Jack's hand dipped under the crop top, and his whole hand was on Tori's breast, separated from flesh by only her bra. Tori's top tented and stretched to accommodate the hand. Alex's heart beat faster, and he looked over at the older lady. Her view was blocked, Alex realized, by Jack leaning forward slightly and by the rise of Tori's other breast. Still, she was frowning.

Another stop; still no one entered. Five stops more to go.

Tori put her hand on Jack's thigh, squeezing him through his slacks. It stayed there for just a moment, before Tori placed it directly on Jack's crotch. Alex had no doubt that Tori could feel Jack's cock, and that his cock was hard.

The door opened and a younger man came in. College kid, Alex guessed, since he boarded at the stop next to the university. He raised his eyebrows when he saw Tori and Jack. Alex imagined what he saw: Tori's legs apart to show her panties, her hand on Jack's dick, and Jack's hand on her tit. Alex imagined what he was thinking: that Tori was a slut, and that Jack was a damned lucky guy. The college kid sat across the aisle from Jack and Tori. It was the seat with the best view of the action. The college kid's choice of seating seemed to be the last straw for the old lady, who got up with a undisguised huff and walked away, finding a seat facing away from everybody.

Tori made eye contact with the boy, and bit her lip. Alex couldn't tell whether she was really embarrassed, or just putting on an act. She kept her hand on Jack's hard cock, though. Alex realized that his own cock was hard, too, and had been for a while.

Everyone sat there frozen, for a minute. The door opened, closed. No one got on. Three more stops.

Tori gave Jack's cock a parting squeeze as she removed her hand. The kid's eyes bulged. Alex wondered if the kid thought Tori was really a teenager. He hoped things were going to calm down a little. His dick had gotten painfully hard.

He should have known, did know at some level, that Jack wasn't going to let things calm down. Jack followed Tori's glance and looked the college kid up and down. Then he moved his hand, the one that was resting on Tori's thigh, up under her skirt. Tori's eyes widened. Alex wondered what Jack was doing there, if he was fingering her or rubbing her, if his hand was inside or outside her panties. He wanted to get up and stop them, or at least take the college kid's seat and get a better view.

Jack said something to Tori. The boy could hear every word, Alex was sure, but Alex could hear only that the sentence started with "Vicki," and sounded like a command. Tori snuggled up close to Jack, pressing her unoccupied tit against his chest. The movement did nothing to move Jack's hand away from her cunt, but it did turn her bottom toward Alex and caused the skirt in front to flip down more decently.

The door opened and closed, but no came in and Alex hardly noticed the old lady get off. He wanted to know whether Jack's hand was inside his wife. His cock was so hard that it hurt. He wondered if stroking himself was permitted, and decided reluctantly that it wasn't. *Sit still,* Jack had said, with Tori nodding.

Tori squirmed up against Jack as if she was trying to make sure he rubbed her in just the right place. In the process she raised her bottom, and her skirt rode up. Tori seemed unaware of this, but Alex caught a glimpse of her panties. They were pink.

Jack's hand moved within Tori's top, and quite obviously squeezed her nipple. Tori gasped. The kid's eyes widened. Jack let go of Tori's tit and moved his hand down to clutch her ass. He looked amused to find Tori's skirt already conveniently out of the way. Tori wrapped her arms around Jack's neck and kissed his ear and the side of his neck passionately.

They pulled into the penultimate station and Alex noticed a policeman walking along the platform. They could get arrested, Alex realized. He got out of his seat, ready to dive in front of Tori and Jack if that would do any good. His mouth opened to shout out a warning.

The cop passed by and got into another subway car, and Alex sat back down without saying anything. Neither Jack nor Tori noticed his infraction, although the college kid did. Of course, thought Alex, he doesn't know it was an infraction. Heck, he doesn't even know I'm involved.

Jack let Tori go. "Take 'em off, Vicki," he told her, plenty loud.

Tori stood up, took a nervous look around, reached under her skirt, and slipped her panties out from under. She handed them to Jack. The kid's eyes were wide.

"You've got a wet snatch," said Jack. "What are you going to do to make it happy?"

"Find somebody to fuck, I guess," said Tori.

"How 'bout him?" asked Jack, pointing to the college kid. "Show him your pussy."

Tori turned around to face the boy and lifted her skirt. The kid just stared, and mumbled something that Alex couldn't make out. Alex's heart beat fast. They're taking it too far, he thought. She's my wife.

Jack smiled. "You're such a slut," he said to Tori. She turned back to Jack, letting her skirt drop back into place. She was blushing.

Tori pointed over at Alex. "I wanna fuck *him*. May I, please?"

"Of course, Vicki. As long as you fuck *some* stranger, you know we'll both be happy."

Tori smoothed her skirt down just as the train was slowing down. Jack tucked the panties into his pants pocket. The college kid's eyes followed Tori's every move as she walked to Alex, smiled at him, and held out her hand. Alex took her hand, and rose from his seat. He put a hand around her waist, his pinky finger resting on the familiar first curve of her bottom.

The doors opened. Jack got up, nodded to the kid, and looked over at Alex and Tori. Tori didn't notice. Jack winked, and Alex smiled. Tori and Alex followed Jack out the door, but Jack headed for a different exit. They would talk on the phone later.

The kid left last, if he left at all. Alex imagined him sitting on the train for a while, playing it all back in his mind.

They walked to their car, a blue two-door Toyota Tercel, in silence. The parking lot was dark and almost deserted, only a few cars left at this late hour. As they walked, Alex's hand slowly slid lower, feeling Tori's ass through her skirt.

"You drive," he said. If he drove he knew he would be distracted from the road by the hard ache of his cock.

"Oh, honey," said Tori. Her voice was husky. "I'm so turned on, I don't know if I can drive safely."

He unlocked the driver's-side door. Tori stood next to him, her breast pressing against his arm. He felt her move, and looked over to see her rubbing her hand against the front of her skirt.

He opened the door, tilted the front seat forward, and crawled into the backseat. He had barely sat down when Tori crawled on top of him, straddling him with her bare thighs. He instantly felt the moist heat of her pantyless crotch through the thin fabric of his pants.

She grabbed the door, slammed it closed. Alex hurried to pull the crop top over her head, hoping it would tear. Tori unfastened the bra and let it fall to the plush floor of the car. They heard a car engine and froze for a moment while the headlights of the car illuminated Tori's bare torso for a moment. The car drove on.

Alex took a tit in his mouth, sucking hard, almost biting on the already turgid nipple. Tori worked the zipper of his jeans, her fingers made clumsy from haste. Finally, his cock was freed, springing out stiff as a board, radiating heat. He lifted Tori just enough that her slit hovered above the head of it. She settled over him like a smooth glove, her skirt covering his thighs. She was so wet. He didn't know which of them was more aroused.

He thrust into her hard, repeatedly, bucking her almost off and then pulling her to him with his strong hands gripping her ass. They were caught in the lights from another pair of headlights, suddenly, and these lingered, as if whoever was in the car was watching.

Tori screamed in pleasure, her cunt tightening around him, pulsing. In response, Alex exploded inside her, gasping. They held each other, not looking around, until the car drove off.

Alex realized how very much in love he was with his wife. He told her so.

"I love you, too, honey," said Tori. "I was thinking the whole time how much I was going to enjoy being in bed with you when we got home." She giggled. "We didn't make it home, did we?"

"No," agreed Alex.

"One question, honey?"

"Hmm?"

"Jack's throwing a party in a couple of nights. He and I have some wicked ideas. Can we go?"

A Walk in the Park

MARIE SUDAC

I know something's going to happen; I just don't know what. You've asked me to go on my daily walk through the park, but today you told me to wear your favorite skirt. It's something sexy, but not too obvious—a prim silk number that falls to midthigh, deepest burgundy to match my lipstick and to contrast the forest-green blouse that's just a little more low-cut in front than my usual. Comfortable shoes, but with something of a heel.

Anyone seeing me walk through the park here at the cusp of darkness would think I was only a businesswoman who hadn't changed out of her work clothes before going on a little stroll through the park. They might see the sparkle in my eye, but it probably wouldn't mean anything to them. They wouldn't know about the tight, see-through black thong on over my garters, or the lace tops to my sheer, seamed black stockings. Or the lacy bra under my form-fitting blouse. You didn't ask for those; they were my innovation.

The park is deserted, though, and there's nobody to walk by me and not know. The smell of the pines and the dust invigorates me; it was a hot day, and it's just now cooling down. It feels great. I stretch in the low-slanting sunlight and take deep breaths of the clean air, glad to be out.

I don't take much notice when I hear the car behind me. I don't notice the four men inside—two in back, two in front. Not until the big white sedan pulls in front of me, just in front of me, and the doors pop open. Suddenly there's one guy in front of me and one behind me—big men, one black and one maybe Latino.

I'm about to say their names. But the one behind me speaks first, as he crowds up behind me.

"Hello, girl—you look good enough to eat! You want to take a little ride?"

It takes me only an instant to figure out what game you've got in mind. I scowl and try to squirm away from the men.

"No, thanks, I'll walk," I say, and instinctively reach for my whistle. The guy in front of me grabs it out of my hand, bends forward to grab my other wrist as I move to slap him. He's good-looking, beefy, and Latin, and it's as if I'm noticing him for the first time, as if I don't know him. He takes my whistle and puts it in his pocket.

"What d'you need that for, lady? Four nice guys want to take you for a ride, why d'you have to make problems? Most ladies would do a lot to get a date from four good-lookin' gents like us."

I struggle against him as they push me toward the car. There's an instant when I almost have to laugh, it all seems so perfect. But I manage to suppress it and succumb to the instinctive fright as I'm pushed into the back seat, the black man forcing me over to the middle, where I'm shoved against an equally big, scary-looking, and familiar white guy. He grins at me wolfishly as the black man gets in behind me, slamming the door, and the Latino guy gets in front. I see *you* there, driving, not turning around to look at me, as if you don't even care what's happening. You hit the gas and pull away, heading into what remains of the setting sun. Only a few more minutes and it'll be dark.

Now no one's holding my wrists, but the two men in the back seat are sitting so close that I couldn't move much if I tried. The feeling of body heat against me sends a surge through my body; in fact, I know if I slipped my finger up there I would be gushing-wet already. That's how fast you've worked your magic on me. The white guy takes my hand and leans close, smiling at me; I can smell the whiskey and cigarettes on his breath. The black man's arms are around me; he's kissing the back of my neck.

"What's your name?" asks the white guy.

"Ur…Ursula," I say, too frightened and stunned to lie.

"Ursula what?"

"Why do you want to know my name?"

"Just tell me, Ursula. That's such a pretty name. Ursula what?"

"Ursula Parker," I tell him, and he leans close to kiss me. I close my lips tight and he starts kissing my ear, sucking on the lobe. The black man is biting the back of my neck now, hungrily, as if devouring me. I can feel his arms around me, his hands coming up to cup my breasts. I try to pull his hands off me, but he grabs them both and forces my palms over my own tits. He's very strong.

"Ursula Parker," says the white guy. "That's a beautiful name...just like you. My name's Jason. That's Mike feeling up your tits, and there in the front's Eric, and Charlie's driving." They're new names, unfamiliar, stranger's names, which only makes me hotter. "You're gonna get to know us a whole lot better than that, Ursula Parker."

I try to pull my hand free but the white guy grabs it and places it on his crotch, firmly holding it there. His cock is big and hard against his tight jeans.

"See what you do to me, Ursula?" he whispers breathily into my ear. "You're a very beautiful woman. You're gonna have a great time with us four studs."

"Let me go," I say, trying to push him away, trying to struggle, but Mike has my wrists and as I squirm he pulls my arms back behind me, roughly, and pins them there. Jason grabs my hair and twists, pulling me down into his lap so that Mike can get a better hold on my wrists while I feel thick rope encircle them.

I feel him knotting the ropes expertly—he's done this many times before. If this was real I would wonder how many women my age or younger have sat here between these two street toughs and felt their hands and mouths on their bodies; now, I know it's just me, and that sends a surge of excitement and fear through me as I feel the ropes cinching tight.

Mike and Jason pull/push me back upright, and now I'm squirming in the seat with nothing to give me purchase, no seat belt, nothing but their bodies against me holding me up as you take the curves of the park roads faster and faster. We're heading up to the observation point, heading up the back way where nobody goes. Knowing that makes me breathe harder. Jason's face is close to mine, smiling as he kisses the side of my neck; meanwhile, I feel Mike's hands on my breasts, massaging them enough to feel the nipples hard through the silk blouse. I feel him pinching my nipples, rolling them between thumb and forefinger, and I feel a wave of heat go from my tits to my rapidly flooding pussy. I look at him, eyes wide, looking scared, staring into his dark, comforting eyes as he strokes my breasts.

Then he starts unbuttoning my blouse.

"Don't," I say, and he says, "Shhhhhhh," taking each button one at a time, slowly exposing the full swell of my pale cleavage and the ephemeral lace of the sexy bra. He whistles in approval and says "I like a girl who knows how to dress sexy." He gets my shirt open all the way, and now I know he can see my nipples, obvious and hard, through the see-through gauze of the black bra. He gently works the cups down over my teacup breasts and bends down to kiss them, taking my nipples in his mouth. The warmth soothes me, and I only squirm a little as his tongue flickers roughly over my hard nipples; besides, the little bit I do squirm is nullified by Jason's arms holding my shoulders, making sure I don't try to get away.

"There, isn't that nice?" Jason says, his breath hot on my ear as he pulls my blouse over my shoulders. Mike unhooks the front-clasp of my bra and peels the sweaty mesh back, Jason holding me tight in case I freak out. Then Jason's bending down low, his mouth finding one breast while Mike suckles the other. I lean back and feel their hot tongues working in tandem to send shivers through my body. I can feel it in my clit, a hard throbbing that surges double every time one of them presses his tongue against the tip of my nipple. Now I'm squirming but good, and I hear my lips uttering, "Oh God, oh God, oh God" before I can stop myself.

Then Jason's mouth is on mine, hard this time, not taking no for an answer. I can't close my lips before his tongue is in my mouth, pressing it open, stroking my own. He savages my mouth with his, and I don't even try to stop him any more, just recline against his body while he slips his hand into my hair and holds me tight so that I won't get away. I feel Mike's hands on my breasts, squeezing hard this time, thumbs and forefingers working my nipples roughly enough to make me squeal if I could—but I can't, I just lie there and feel Jason taking possession of my mouth. They own me now, and they know it; however much I might struggle, Mike and Jason know they'll have me any and every way they want. That's true long before Mike works his hand between my thighs, under my skirt. I try to clamp my legs shut, try to pull against the ropes and get free so that I can push his hand away, but it's useless; he struggles against me, unyielding and vehement, forcing my knees apart and pulling my ass over on the seat so that he can put his body weight on my knees and hold me open. I hear Mike saying, "Shhhhhh, Ursula, don't fight, just let it happen, it's going to happen whether you like it or not, you may as well enjoy it," and I feel Jason's hand on my breasts. Now I'm stretched between Mike and Jason, Mike holding my legs down and open, my head cradled in Jason's arms as he kisses me, my hair gripped in his powerful fist while his other hand caresses my tits.

Mike's hand travels under my skirt and he feels the thong, feels it soaked with my juices, slips his finger underneath the crotch and into me. I can feel a dribble of liquid running out; I hear Mike chuckling.

"Don't even try to play hard-to-get now, Ursula," he says, and he pulls my skirt all the way up, tucking it over my waist as his hands work around my hips and force their way under my ass, getting hold of the thong. "Thong panties, shaved puss, and you are the wettest girl I ever had the pleasure of feeling. When a girl's gonna try to play virgin, she wears boxers. You must need this pretty bad." He lets my thighs come together and he pulls the thong down, past my knees, past my calves, over my ankles. He cranks the windows down and tosses them out onto the park road. "You look better without them, anyway," he says.

This time it's short work getting my legs open, since I know I can't resist. I can feel Jason's hand working under my head and hear the rattling of his belt buckle as he undoes it. I know what's coming next, and my mouth is watering so much I couldn't say no if I tried, but saying no is half the fun. He's still got hold of my hair, and he guides my face down into his crotch as he pulls his hard cock out of his pants. "Come on," he says. "I know you know how." That's all it takes, and I hardly even know I'm doing it. My mouth is around his cock, hard against my tongue and thick in the back of my throat, and if I had hands free I'd be rubbing myself and coming right about now.

But then, Mike is taking care of that. He's got two fingers inside me, slowly pumping in and out, and I shudder every time he hits my G-spot. He keeps up the slow rhythm as he lets the thumb of his other hand join its brothers in my pussy, just for a second, making me gasp as my pussy is stretched wide. But he's just getting it wet, a fact I don't realize until I feel his thumb sliding between my cheeks and working its way up against my anus. I don't stop sucking Jason's cock for an instant; it's an awkward position without any hands, but my hunger for his cock has become so intense that it's all of one piece, the fingers in my cunt mirroring the hunger for cock in my mouth. I can hear Jason moaning as I take him all the way down, filling my throat with him and holding it deep for as long as I can stand it without breathing. I squirm even more now as I feel Mike's thumb forcing its way into my ass, against the flesh that's so tight at first, then hungry and yielding as it gives way and accepts his thick thumb. That's when I come, hard, pumping Jason's cock into my mouth as my cunt and asshole spasm around Mike's hands. "Oh, yeah," coos Mike. "You've been needing this, little girl, haven't you, Ursula?"

The car is thick with male sweat and pre-cum. It's so hot in here I'm slicked with sweat myself, mine and Mike's and Jason's. I'm slippery as an eel.

Jason's let go of my hair, now, his hands caressing my breasts and pinching the nipples as Mike gets his pants open. It's obvious I don't need to be controlled; my hunger for cock has taken me over, and I'm an expert. Jason pinches my nipples harder as he comes, his cock jetting sharp semen into my mouth and down my throat. I swallow as much as I can, sucking on his cock as he finishes and it softens quickly. Then I feel it: the thick head of Mike's cock against my vulva, teasing me, working my lips open. His thumb's still in my back door, and he's using it like a handle to make sure he can control where my crotch goes. Even in this big car there's not much room in a backseat; one of my ankles is up against the back window and the other is tucked under the front seat. Mike is turned to one side and his cock just reaches me, making me gasp as he enters me.

Jason is easing me out of his lap, getting out of the car. I realize we've stopped; with the door open I can smell the eucalyptus that tells me we're at the very summit, probably the back part of it, totally hidden from patroling cops or passersby—most of the time. Jason slams the door closed and Mike slips his cock out of me, loses his shirt, and climbs onto me, my wrists wedged under my body, which would be uncomfortable if he didn't put his hand in my hair and grip tight as he mounts me, making sure my head doesn't slip back and hit the door. I wonder if Eric is going to take his turn or if they'll let Mike have me all to himself for a minute. Then all that's gone and Mike is entering me again, his cock feeling so much bigger at this angle, filling me up as he forces his thumb into my mouth. I taste the muskiness of my own asshole and feel momentarily embarassed that it propels a wave of arousal through me just as I feel Mike's cock reach my deepest point, his cockhead grinding against my cervix. My G-spot feels swollen, engorged, more sensitive than it's ever been, and I know I'm going to come again before he's through with me. His naked chest is wet all over, his sweat dripping on my face and breasts; I open my mouth wide and feel it hitting my tongue like salty summer rain. God, these guys should get Oscars, or maybe Tonys. As he looks down into my open mouth, he lets a ball of spit form between his pursed lips and it hits me, square on the tongue, tasteless and overwhelming. I feel the warm liquid sliding down my throat and look up at Mike, more hungry than ever for him.

Mike begins to fuck me, slowly at first, then harder and faster as he senses that I like having my cervix pounded. I'm squealing now, for real, my whole body alive with the sensations as Mike's cock fills me. His muscled body works faster and faster as he forces his mouth against mine, his tongue sliding in deep as I rise toward my second orgasm.

The door comes open. "Hey, is it standing-room-only in there?"

"Rumor has it she likes it in both holes," says Mike. "All three, actually. You really went to town on Jason's cock, Ursula."

"Oh, that's sweet," says Eric. "I've been needing to have my knob polished. She does it real good?"

"Fuck," I hear Jason's voice, outside, wafting in on the smell of cigarette smoke. "I ain't never had a suck-job that good. She'll fuckin' suck the enamel right off your teeth."

"Just don't *you* start suckin' it," says Eric, the four of them chuckling and enjoying their little homophobic joke, and the rush of male-bonding energy is so intense it almost makes me come. I'm being used, I realize, used like a buffer between these men, to get their needs met and prove they're as tough as one another. Then Mike's cock slams into me again and he pulls himself up half-onto his haunches, scrunching forward as Eric gets hold of my shoulders and pulls me over to the edge of the car seat, my head hanging out upside down now as he gets his pants open and leans down low, one hand against the roof of the car, the other on my face, thumb working open my mouth so that he knows I'm wide open and ready for him—as if I could possibly say no, now, in this position, hovering on the brink of a second orgasm twice as intense as the first. Best of all, with Mike leaning back like that he can reach down and rub his thumb against my clit, and I'm moaning in mindless, savage desperation by the time I feel Eric's cock on my tongue. If I could grab it and force it deeper I would, but he controls everything, and he only gives me half, now, making sure I don't choke, one faint warp in the fabric of this reality they've created. But once he knows I can handle it, he pushes deeper, and I take a deep breath just in time to feel his cock against the entrance to my throat; he feels as if he's going to pull back, but I give a sudden excited whimper and he gets the message: I feel him entering my throat smoothly, in one gentle thrust, until my nose is against his balls and I inhale deeply of his scent. He does it another couple of times very, very slowly, and each time I whimper and nod slightly to let him know it's OK, taking deep breaths between thrusts. That's when he starts in earnest, his hips pumping and forcing his cock rhythmically into my throat. I have to time my breaths perfectly, but I've had a lot of practice—this is one of the favorite games you and I play, you fucking me like this. Now I'm just a passive receiver, and knowing he's going to do this to me until he comes makes me relax into the feel of two men inside me, both deep, both pumping, straining, striving. That's when I realize how close I am to coming. Right on the brink, in fact, because in this position Mike's cockhead is rubbing my G-spot mercilessly, and his thumb is on my clit. I don't know how I keep breathing in the right rhythm as my body explodes in orgasm, but I do—and I can feel Eric enjoying me just as much as Mike for every instant of my intense orgasm.

But they both stop pumping as I finish, and they're both chuckling. "You thinking what I'm thinking?" says Eric, and Mike pulls his dripping cock out of my pussy, Eric out of my mouth, dribbling saliva down over my face. Out comes the knife, and I've been so totally engulfed that I don't feel an instant's fear. They cut the ropes around my wrists and pull me out of the car, stripping off my blouse and bra and leaving them, discarded, in the dirt. Eric holds me and kisses my neck while Mike bends down and removes my skirt. Now I'm naked except for the garter belt, stockings, and shoes, and I feel Mike pushing me up against the side of the car and holding me there while a bright flash goes off, then another, then another. Polaroids: They're documenting my disgrace to jerk off to later. The only thing that makes it hotter is seeing the face dancing in my eyes amid the sparkling blue afterglow: You, grinning wide with a lit cigarette dangling out of the corner of your mouth, and, I see when I look down, the shadow of your cock illuminated huge and hard in the reflection off the lake.

Mike pushes me over to the front of the car, where he leans back on the hood and bends me forward. Eric's in front of me, his pants still open, his cock still hard, his arms around me to support me as I lean as far forward as I can go. I realize what they're planning as soon as I feel the cold squirt of lubricant in my crack, feel Mike's thumb massaging me open.

Oh God, can I really take them both? I have been brought under so far that I can't possibly even utter the question, just open wide and accept everything that is done to me. Mike pulls me into his lap, lifting me with Eric's help so that he can fit his lube-slicked cockhead between my cheeks. My eyes go wide and I almost choke as I feel it entering me, but he goes slow. I clench my muscles and then relax as I wriggle myself down; with a sudden surge, I feel the thick cockhead pop into me, feel my body sliding slowly down the shaft as Eric and Mike release me. *Oh God,* I think. *It's really in my ass.* I almost can't believe it went in so smoothly, and it feels incredible there. But there's still more cock to be had.

Eric takes off his shirt and pulls his pants down to his ankles so that he can get at me better. Now that I'm sitting in Mike's lap with his cock in my ass, I'm at the perfect height for Eric's frame. He spreads my yielding legs and gets his cock between my pussy lips; then he slides it home and I see stars as I'm filled fuller than ever.

Moaning between their straining, sweating bodies, I reach down and begin to rub my clit. Eric snatches my wrist and pulls it away, saying, "Let me do that, Ursula. Your cunt's gonna feel so good around my cock when you come." He starts rubbing, and it's as if he's known my body for years, knows exactly how to make me come. Jason is there, next to us, his cock out and hard again as he works it in his fist. I meet his eyes with mine and beckon him in with my opened mouth; he crowds over to us and climbs onto the hood of the car. I catch a glimpse of you, watching, smiling, and smoking in the dark, and I beckon to you with my hand, wanting one more hard cock to satisfy me. But you just shake your head and stand there. Then Jason thrusts his cock in my face, and I take it in my mouth, tasting the residue of cum from the last time I sucked it. That doesn't deter me a bit, nor does it slow Jason down. The three sweating bodies pump into me, filling everything I have to be filled except the need to have you with me. But for now, I can't even think about that; I'm too busy feeling Mike fuck his way into my wide-open ass, Eric close in on his orgasm, and Jason grasp my hair so that he can pump his hips, working his cock into my mouth with a familiar rhythm. I've got one hand around the base of Jason's cock, trying to milk him into my mouth. But it's Eric who comes first, pumping into my cunt and shooting inside me. I moan "Yeah, yeah" as he comes, and when he pulls out I feel Mike getting ready to do it. I usually don't like you to come inside my ass, but this time it's all I've ever wanted to feel to have Mike's cum jetting into my back door. He holds my hips, bouncing me up and down so that the whole car squeaks and wobbles in time with our fucking. Then he's grunting, and my ass is so tight around his cock that I can feel him injecting me, his cock spasming deep inside, the warmth flooding me. Jason's ready to come, too, and I pump his cock with my hand so that I can taste each jet of him as he comes in my mouth.

Slowly they pull themselves away from me, leaving me dripping their semen and covered in their sweat. My hair is tangled from having it pulled so much, and my throat and pussy and mouth all ache, raw and reddened. I am more sated than I ever have been in my life. But when they ease me to my feet and I see you standing there, smiling, holding my dirt-smeared clothes up for me to get dressed, I don't hesitate for an instant; I know what I have to do.

I'm down on my knees in the dirt before you know what's happening. You start to protest as I push you back against the hood of the car, and your belt comes open easily in my hand. I hear the three men around us chuckling, making comments about how now that I've been "broken in" all I want to do is suck cock. But they know when to keep their distance.

I unzip your pants and find you hard, ready for me. I take you in my mouth and it feels as if I'm going to come again as a shudder goes through my body. How can your cock taste so different than all the others? How can it practically make me come from touching my tongue, how can the taste of it fill me with such satisfaction? Because you're the lover who would orchestrate this for me, who would arrange my abduction with our three closest friends, a triad of gay men who, I guess, are more bi than they ever let on. And this cock in my mouth is the cock that spawned it all, the filthy, hard organ that guides all your dirtiest, darkest fantasies for me.

I want to suck you forever, but I can feel how turned on you are. It's as if you didn't want to let me know, didn't want to spoil the focus, didn't want it to be about *you* getting off, rather than me. But you getting off is what gets *me* off, and for this last, pyrotechnic orgasm we're both going to come if it's the last thing we do. Down on my knees with my legs spread wide, sharp rocks cutting into my flesh, I can massage your balls with one hand while I rub my clit with the other, all the while sucking you with a hunger that surprises even me. You're going to come, you're going to come so soon, and I want the sensation of exploding with my final orgasm while I feel your cock letting go inside me.

I slip your cock out of my mouth, drool raining on my hand and arm as I lave the underside with my tongue, panting hot and hard all over it. "Come for me," I whisper as I rub my clit. "Come in my mouth, 'Charlie.' "

Then it's one quick roll of your cock against my cheek, the texture silky and slick with spit, and I'm back on you, my mouth holding you tight, pumping up and down on your cock as I rush toward climax, rubbing my clit but trying to hold off until you start to come—and then you let out a groan and I feel the jet on my tongue, and it doesn't even take another stroke of my hand before my whole body is consumed in my own orgasm, like ocean waves rushing over me, drowning me like your salty cum.

When we both finish, I lick you all over one more time, licking you clean. I tuck your cock into your underwear, zip your jeans, buckle your belt. I look up at you, a woman in love, down on her knees, and if I ever wondered how lucky I am, now I know.

You hold out my blouse.

I shake my head, slowly slink to my feet, and kiss you. "Drive me home naked," I tell you, my body sweaty against yours. "For that matter, let someone else drive."

Sailor Boy
ALISON TYLER

To me, the term *macho* means masculine. Powerful. Butch.
Given this definition, the word doesn't even begin to describe
my husband, Alexander. Tall and strong, he has a deep, commanding voice that resonates when he talks, vibrates inside
my head when he says my name. I like to watch him move, to
watch him stride. When he cuts through a crowd, people move
out of his way.

Before we met, Alexander was a commercial fisherman,
spending eight rough years at work on a variety of vessels. He
lived thirty days at sea at a time, followed by one-week breaks
on land. He credits his time aboard ship for building his spirit,
his mind, his body. At sea, Alex came across as the toughest
of the bunch. There were no women on the fishing boats—
chicks on board are considered bad luck—and there was no
sexual activity among the men (at least, none that anyone

would admit to if they wanted to be hired for a second trip). To get the reputation for liking guys meant instant unemployment in the fishing game. But while Alex fulfilled his he-man duties, he lost himself in a forbidden fantasy. One that didn't come true until he met me.

Many husbands give their wives perfume on February 14th, but my handsome sailor boy gave me something with a twist. Not Chanel Number Five, Joy, or Anaïs Anaïs, but a fancy brand of men's cologne. "Happy Valentine's Day, Becky," he whispered as I tore through the heart-printed wrapping paper to reveal the expensive bottle. I looked at it, looked at Alex, and smiled. I knew exactly what my one true love wanted from Cupid, and I wasn't about to let him down.

Alex has gray-green eyes that change when he stares at me. They grow darker, more turbulent, like a storm at sea. As I began to rub the spicy lotion into the soft skin at the base of my throat, his eyes shimmered with desire and longing.

"Get undressed," I said, motioning with my chin toward the bedroom. "Strip out of your clothes and then wait for me."

He couldn't hide his grin, but he ducked his head, bashfully, and then followed my command. Wives tend to know their husbands, sometimes better than the men know themselves. I'd been planning for this day for a long time, and I felt excitement pool within me. What a surprise Alex was in for—he thought he knew the evening's plans, but he had no idea. After he'd left the room, I stood and got the secret present I'd been saving for him. Quickly, I pulled out the leather harness and dildo, then grabbed an outfit from the back of the hall closet and went into the bathroom to change. Or, rather, to *transform*.

With Alex's unfulfilled fantasy in mind, I had purchased a vintage sailor suit at a second-hand store. It was white with a black anchor on the sleeve and a musky, male smell to the fabric, even though I'd had it dry-cleaned. I hung the outfit on the back of the door while I attached the molded dildo to the harness, then slid the straps on and buckled the leather belt around my waist. The cock was as true-to-life as they come, as close to my actual skin color as possible, and ribbed with realistic veins. In length and girth it matched Alex's almost exactly, which was what I'd wanted. My desire was for him to experience what I get to feel every night.

After admiring my cock in the mirror, and admonishing myself not to get too infatuated with the look of it, I slid into the outfit. First, I put on a tight white tank bra that pressed my small breasts flat to my chest. I pulled the top over my head and then tried on the pants. I'm a slim 5'8", but I'd had the pants altered and they fit perfectly, showing off the newfound bulge in front and my fine, round ass in the back. As I dressed, I imagined Alex's hands unbuttoning the fly, his trembling fingers revealing the molded cock concealed beneath. One that was destined to introduce his virgin ass to the as-yet-inexperienced pleasures of life as a submissive.

I completed my outfit with a pair of beat-up black Doc Martens. Then I slicked my short blonde hair away from my face and gave myself a final once-over. It was my intention to look the part of a boy, yet retain my feminine side, and I felt as if I'd done a perfect job. Still, I took my time with my finishing touches, sure that Alex was squirming in our room, growing harder ever second. He's unused to being out of control, tends to take charge in our relationship—at least, in the bedroom portion of it. I wondered what he was thinking about, whether his heart was beating extra fast from that sexy combination of anticipation and fear.

With more swagger to my stride than normal, I walked out of the bathroom and down the hall to our bedroom. Alex likes to tease me, says that I always walk as if I'm going somewhere, even when we're out for a leisurely stroll. Now, I definitely had a purpose. Each step brought me further into my character. Long ago, Alex had confessed to being attracted to one of the cooks who had worked on a boat with him. He claimed the boy had looked like me, was of a slighter build than the rest of the burly sailors, with fairly feminine features and a "divine ass." So, now I was Jake Miller, heading into our room to turn a forbidden fantasy into a reality.

I opened the door slowly, seeing that Alex had dimmed the lights and lit the two ivory candles on our dresser. He was sitting on the edge of the bed, wearing a pair of gray cotton boxers, his eyes lowered, his body shaking slightly. I'd never seen him nervous before, never imagined he could appear vulnerable. Now that he was, I had a momentary lapse back into myself, wanting to go on my hands and knees in front of him, take his face in my hands, croon soothing words. But I'd fail him if I did.

Instead, I approached solidly, grabbed his chin in my hand, and forced him to meet my eyes. He didn't want to. He raised his face but kept his eyes lowered, staring at my feet.

"Look at me," I said, my voice low and as gruffly masculine as possible. His body shivered again, and this time he obeyed. "I've seen you watching me," I told him, "seen the way you stare when I walk by. You think about me at night, alone in your bunk, your hand on your cock."

Alex swallowed hard and nodded. My confidence grew inside me. I could feel a heat spreading through my chest.

"You work yourself and imagine that I'm fucking you."

Again, he nodded, his eyes wide. Taking a step closer, I pressed the bulge of my hidden rod directly in front of his mouth.

"You want to taste my cock, don't you?" I asked, my tone still low, barely louder than a whisper.

"Yeah." His mouth was partly open. He looked as if he wanted to deep-throat me right there. I didn't let him, but I rubbed my pants-clad cock against his mouth, taunting him with the tool. He opened his mouth wider, cupping the head of my cock between his lips, wetting the clothing of my pants with his saliva. He looked as if he knew what he was doing, and I felt a surge of wetness in my pussy beneath the plastic prick. I was getting turned on watching his gray-green eyes beg me.

"Unbutton my fly," I told him, savoring the look of gratitude that flickered across his face. He was quick to oblige, undoing the buttons and then sliding the pants down over my hips so that my cock bulged forward. That wasn't good enough for me. I kicked out of the shoes and tore off the pants, so that I had better control of my cock. What a perfect specimen it was, everlastingly erect and ready.

"Suck me," I ordered next, the words not even out of my mouth before his lips were around my new toy. I stroked his soft auburn hair while he made good use of his mouth. I felt the pull of his throat muscles as he tried futilely to drain a plastic cock.

"This is going in your ass," I told him next, and he sighed out loud, around the dildo. "This is going deep in your ass, and you're gonna cry out with each stroke. You're going to whimper like a girl." I didn't know where the words were coming from, but I let them come, did nothing to stifle myself. In reality, there's no way I can force Alex to do anything. He outweighs me by more than fifty pounds, but I just let my body and my mind get into it, not caring that our heights and weights were so disproportionate to the characters we were playing. And as I pulled him off me and motioned for him to take off his boxers and get face-down on the bed, I could tell I'd have no back-talk from him. He *wanted* this. He'd been fantasizing about it for years.

There was a tube of K-Y in the drawer (I'd planned ahead), and I lubed both my cock and his asshole before introducing him to the toy. Gently, I pressed the head of the cock into his asshole, giving him just the first inch. His body tensed, the muscles in his back alive and straining. His head twitched on the pillow, and I could see his reflection in the glass-encased picture over our bed. He was biting his lip, trying to stop himself from moaning.

But I wanted him to moan.

I thrust into him with the full length of the cock, then pulled out quickly, and jogged right back in. Don't ask me how I knew the rhythm, or how I sensed what he needed. I just knew. The way to please my husband was to fuck him hard, to fuck him fast. He wanted to be taken, and I had no problem delivering.

Within a few strokes, he simply couldn't help himself. He leaned his head back and groaned at the feel of it, the intrusion and the sensation of being filled. I liked making him lose himself, and I wanted to keep up the ride. Squatting on my knees on either side of his body, I came back up on my feet for better control. I have very strong thigh muscles, and I used them to really fuck him. Grabbing onto his shoulders for support, I slammed into him with the cock, speaking the whole time, saying, "You like it like that, don't you, Alex? You like it when your boyfriend fucks your ass...."

I took his moans for assents, not asking him to answer me properly. He was so lost in his daydreams that I don't think he would even have heard me if I'd made a demand. Somewhere else in his mind, he was being fucked by his fantasy sailor boy. But I felt no competition. I'm the woman he comes home to, the woman he comes into, and I leaned my body against his and took a deep breath, smelling the cologne more strongly now that my body was growing hotter. Three fragrances permeated the room: the scent of Dolce & Gabbana, the scent of sweat, and the scent of sex.

Alex controlled the rhythm when he was about to climax, taking over from me and bucking his hips against the sheets, forcing himself back onto the whole of my cock, fucking himself with it. He sighed as he came, calling me *Jake,* and then calling me *Becky*, and then smiling as he rolled over and murmuring again, "Happy Valentine's Day...."

"Happy Valentine's Day, baby," I whispered back, knowing that we wouldn't wait for a special occasion to play this kind of game again.

About the Authors

XAVIER ACTON is a motorcycle-riding computer programmer from the San Francisco Bay Area. His writing has appeared on Gothic.Net and Necromantic.com. Club Labyrinth does not really exist, but SF clubsters may recognize it anyway....

HANNE BLANK has never been able to figure out how Persephone could have restrained herself to only six pomegranate seeds. Associate editor of *Sojourner: The Women's Forum* and coeditor of *Scarletletters.com*, she is a widely published writer and editor as well as the author/editor of several books about sex, including *Big Big Love: A Sourcebook on Sex for People of Size and Those Who Love Them*, *Zaftig: Well Rounded Erotica*, and *Best Transgender Erotica*.

ALICE BLUE'S fiction can be found in *Faster Pussycats*, *The Mammoth Book of New Erotica*, and *My Lover, My Friend*.

ANN BLAKELY is the coauthor of *The Other Rules: Never Wear Panties on a Date and Other Tips*. She has also published several erotic short stories in places such as www.goodvibes.com.

P. E. Brink is a librarian who lives in Virginia with his wife of 12 years and their 4-year-old son. He is currently writing an erotic novel set in prerevolutionary France. "The Last Train" is his first published work.

Mark Brooks is the pseudonym of a California technical writer. "Double Vision" is his first published short story.

M. Christian is the author of more than a hundred published short stories, his work being found in *Best Lesbian Erotica, Best Gay Erotica, Best American Erotica,* and many other books and magazines. He's the editor of seven anthologies and the author of a collection of short stories, *Dirty Words.* A collection of his lesbian short stories, *Speaking Parts,* is coming out in 2002. The only thing he likes better than writing is sex.

Dante Davidson is the coauthor of the best-selling DIY S/M and b/d book *Bondage on a Budget* (Masquerade) and the manual *Secrets for Great Sex After Fifty* (Pound Ridge). His short stories have appeared in *Good Vibrations Magazine.*

Kate Dominic is a Los Angeles–based erotica freelancer whose stories appear in *Herotica 6 and 7, Best Lesbian Erotica 2000, Best Women's Erotica 2000 and 2001, Lip Service, Wicked Words I and IV, Strange Bedfellows,* and dozens of other anthologies and magazines under many pen names. A graduate of the University of Wisconsin, she is a former aerospace editor and technical writer. Her first solo collection, *Any 2 People Kissing,* is available from Down There Press.

SELENE DRAKE is a computer programmer and part-time exotic dancer in Buffalo, New York, who enjoys writing erotica for her lover.

ERICA DUMAS'S poetry and fiction has appeared in *Allusion, Calico, Broken Dances, Fear Time,* and *Seduction.* She lives in New York.

R. GAY is a writer in the Midwest who has an uncanny love affair with onions. Writings past and present can be found in *Herotica 7, Love Shook My Heart II, Clean Sheets, Scarlet Letters,* and others.

CELIA O'TOOLE is a happily married mother of two school-aged children who lives in the San Francisco Bay Area. While writing erotica is one of her favorite pastimes (second only to researching it!), she usually writes nonfiction, focusing on personal effectiveness, parenting, and relationships. She has authored one book and numerous articles and essays, and is now working on her second book.

EMILIE PARIS is the author of the novel *Valentine* (Blue Moon), available as an abridged audiotape by Passion Press. Her short stories have appeared in *Batteries Not Included* (Diva) and on the website www.goodvibes.com.

ERIN PIPES is a writer living in California. Her work has appeared in various magazines, including *Bitch* and *Bust.*

CHARLOTTE POPE is a recovering San Francisco Bay Area dot-commer who writes dirty stories and articles to remind herself that there's more to life than coffee. Her work has appeared in *Pump It Up*, *So Do My*, and the forthcoming *Noirotica 4*.

MARIE SUDAC is a dancer, poet, and writer who lives in the Los Angeles area with her lover and two cats. "A Walk in the Park" is her first published work.

ALISON TYLER is the author of thirteen erotic novels, most recently *Learning to Love It* and *Strictly Confidential*. Her short stories have appeared in anthologies such as *Wicked Words 4*, *Guilty Pleasures*, *Noirotica 3*, *Midsummer Night's Dreams*, *Sex Toy Tales*, *The Unmade Bed*, *Bondage*, and *Gone Is the Shame*, as well as in *Playgirl* magazine and on the website www.goodvibes.com.

BILL VICKERS is the nom de plume of a widely published novelist, playwright, and poet. His stories have appeared in several magazines, including *Libido*, *Cupido*, and *Clean Sheets*, as well as in anthologies such as *Best American Erotica*.

ERIC WILLIAMS is a Los Angeles–based writer. His short stories have appeared in several *Penthouse* publications.

KRISTINA WRIGHT is a full-time writer, an award-winning romance novelist, and a lover of all things erotic and romantic. Her erotica has been published in *Best Women's Erotica 2000, Scarlet Letters,* and *Good Vibrations Magazine,* among others. She lives in Virginia with her husband, surrounded by pets and books.

About the Editor

VIOLET BLUE is senior copywriter at Good Vibrations where she writes book and video reviews, which has her watching an awful lot of porn, and reading virtually everything imaginable written about sex. She is a sex columnist and a sex educator, and was the founding editor of the Good Vibrations Magazine. She is the author of two books on oral sex, *How to Go Down on a Woman* and *How to Go Down on a Man*, both forthcoming from Cleis Press. Visit her web site about all things oral, tinynibbles.com. When not on the job, Violet somehow finds time to enjoy her life's other loves—her handsome husband Todd, their gigantic cat, tasty red wines, and technology-based art.